EYE FOR AN EYE

B.D. Prince

Ghastly Press

Ghastly Press – www.ghastlypress.com
B.D. Prince - www.bdprince.com

Publisher's Note: This is a work of fiction. Names, characters, places, and incidents are a product of the author's imagination. Locales and public names are sometimes used for atmospheric purposes. Any resemblance to actual people, living or dead, or to businesses, companies, events, institutions, or locales is completely coincidental.

Eye for an Eye/ B. D. Prince -- 1st ed.
ISBN 979-8-3304-2676-8

Dedication

I dedicate this book to my first reader, number one fan, and partner for life — Deanne. Thank you for your unwavering love and support.

Thanks to all of my beta readers, editors, and encouragers for helping make this book possible.

And to my good friend, great writer, and even better person—Taylor Grant—with whom I shared a common obsession with The Twilight Zone and EC Comics. He was always there to encourage me in my writing and celebrate my successes. Rest in peace, my friend.

If we do an eye for an eye and a tooth for a
tooth, we will be a blind and toothless nation.

– Martin Luther King, Jr.

Contents

Introduction

People ask me all the time where I get my ideas. The honest answer is... everywhere. Sometimes it's from a nightmare. Other times it's an anomaly I stumble across in my travels that makes me go, "Hmm." Often, it's an interesting word or turn of a phrase that, when filtered through my warped imagination, takes on a whole new meaning, and BAM, there's the seed of a new twisted tale.

Committed was inspired by a paranormal investigation I did in 2019 at Eloise Psychiatric Hospital—an abandoned asylum in southeast Michigan. Having grown up in the Detroit area, I was frightfully familiar with the sanitarium's reputation for housing the criminally insane and its rumored abuses of the mentally ill.

In retrospect, this story was also likely influenced by the many Twilight Zone episodes, EC Comics revenge tales, and black-and-white films that helped shape my love for genre fiction. In particular, films like *Gaslight*, which is where we get the term *gaslighting*, and the many films it inspired, like the classic *Diabolique*, and a film that haunted me as a child, *Hush...Hush, Sweet Charlotte*, featuring the legendary actress, Bette Davis. Hence, the protagonist's name, Charlotte Davis.

The second novella in the collection, *Eye for an Eye*, drew its inspiration from a road trip I took from California to Texas. Particularly those long stretches of desolate highway with enigmatic crossroads that seemingly led to nowhere. Where did they go, and what kind of people lived in the mysterious towns at the other end of those apparently deserted roads?

But the main catalyst behind *Eye for an Eye* was a small Texas town where I noticed that everyone, even the young people, seemed to be missing some or all of their teeth. Was this the meth capital of Texas, or was there something more sinister afoot? That's when the phrase from Leviticus popped in my head—*Eye for an eye, tooth for a tooth*. And the story was born.

Both titles were chosen for their ability to be taken literally and metaphorically. But it wasn't until I went back to edit these two tales that I noticed the common theme (eye for an eye) and the many parallels.

I discovered common themes of injustice, survival, and revenge. Then there was the fun contrast between the 1950s housewife in *Committed* and the Gen-Z college sophomores.

Each story also, quite literally, features eyes. Whether it's Charlotte's husband's wandering eye, the many tears she shed, or the more shocking events in each that I won't spoil here.

The more I thought about it, the more I realized that these two novellas belonged together. Thus, was born... *Eye for an Eye*.

-B.D. Prince

Committed

Charlotte Davis whisked the feather duster across her teak coffee table as she hummed "Love is a Many-Splendored Thing." She couldn't get the song out of her head since the film premiered last month.

Reaching to clear a short stack of magazines from the table, she froze at the sight of Sophia Loren staring up at her from the cover of Life magazine. She could've sworn she'd already stowed it in the magazine rack. But there it was, right in front of Jack's chair.

Charlotte picked up the magazine only to discover another magazine with Grace Kelly gazing coyly over her shoulder. She remembered how Jack couldn't stop talking about her for weeks after "Rear Window" played at the picture show last year. He kept going on and on about how elegant she was and how *Grace* was the perfect name for her. The way he gushed about the actress made Charlotte feel like just another *Plain Jane*.

It probably shouldn't have been such a shock, having found Playboy magazines in the garage a few months back. But when she'd confronted him, he hadn't seemed ashamed or embarrassed in the slightest. Instead, he'd deftly parried her attack using his marketing executive job as an excuse. *Research*, he called it. She ultimately made a deal that as long as he agreed to look but not touch, she wouldn't make a fuss. And then, only if he promised not to bring them into the house.

The shrill ring of the telephone startled Charlotte, nearly causing her to fling the magazine across the room. She hurriedly stuffed the magazines back into their wooden rack and rushed to the kitchen. Her neighbor Joan was already talking before the earpiece reached her ear.

"Did you hear about the Jeffersons?"

Before Charlotte could respond, Joan answered her own question.

"...Bill just ran off with his secretary! Can you believe it?"

Charlotte grabbed a chair from the kitchen table to keep her knees from giving out. The Jeffersons had seemed so happy together. They'd been married nearly as long as she and Jack. Maybe he'd gotten the seven-year itch like in that Marilyn Monroe movie. Was that really a thing, or just a Hollywood invention?

Jack and Charlotte were going on ten years of matrimony. Was he overdue to scratch his seven-year itch? Or was he scratching it behind her back? Charlotte struggled to shake the thought from her head.

"Poor Claire. I can't imagine how she must feel!" Charlotte lamented.

But on reflection, hadn't there been signs? How Bill always kissed the ladies when he greeted them. And last Fourth of July, when the drinks were flowing freely, and she caught Bill staring at her as if he had x-ray eyes. The way he stood too close in the food line. And later that evening, when his wife Alice was looking for him, and nobody seemed to know where he and the divorcee down the street had disappeared to.

"Remember the time," Joan continued, "when I told you that I'd seen his car parked at the motel out on State Street at noontime, and you said I was imagining things?"

"You like to think you know people." Charlotte retrieved a pack of cigarettes from the table, shook one out, and lit it. "How is Claire doing? Have you spoken with her?"

"She's devastated, of course. Her mother is coming to stay with her for a few days."

Charlotte exhaled a stream of smoke, shaking her head. *How well did she really know Jack?*

Joan filled her in on the rest of the neighborhood gossip, but Charlotte only half listened, unable to shake the feeling of betrayal. It wasn't just empathy for Claire; it felt like Bill Jefferson had betrayed the whole neighborhood.

Glancing at the clock, Charlotte stubbed out her cigarette in a glass ashtray. Jack would be home soon and she hadn't even thought about dinner. When Joan paused long enough to take a drag on her cigarette, Charlotte seized the opportunity to end the call.

"Okay, well, I guess I'd better get dinner started for Jack so he doesn't decide to leave me, too," she laughed nervously.

* * *

Charlotte tied her apron around her waist and got to work on dinner. She preheated the oven and pulled a beef roast out of the refrigerator before dusting it with Lipton onion soup mix, just the way Jack liked it. The way his mother always made it. And how Charlotte had made it since he pointed that out during their first week of marriage.

Once the roast was in the oven, she began peeling potatoes over the sink. There was no question that Jack was a meat and potatoes man.

And a ladies' man, Marilyn Monroe's voice cooed inside her head.

The potato peeler slipped, shaving the skin off the side of her index finger. Charlotte dropped the peeler in the sink and quickly ran her finger under some cold water. She watched the bright red blood fade to pink as it swirled down the drain. Fading just like her marriage.

* * *

Charlotte sat at the dining room table, staring at the dinner she'd spent hours preparing growing cold.

She checked the clock on the wall again. Jack should've been home over an hour ago.

Charlotte picked at the green beans. By now, they were so cold that she wondered why she even bothered to boil them.

Another thirty minutes passed. Where could Jack be? Did he have to work late again? Was he stranded on the side of the road changing a flat tire?

At the motel out on State Street?

A tear rolled down her cheek, and she whisked it away.

Charlotte finally fixed herself a plate and ate it cold. Seemed fitting.

As she placed the last bite into her mouth, the roar of an engine and the familiar squeak of brakes announced Jack's arrival.

This had better be good.

Jack came through the front door with a sigh. She waited while he set down his briefcase, hung up his hat and overcoat, and strolled past the dining room.

"Where have you been?" Charlotte asked, unable to conceal the quiver in her voice.

He continued into the kitchen and retrieved a beer from the refrigerator. "I got tied up at work."

"Why didn't you call? Don't you realize how worried you made me?"

"Time just got away from me, I guess." Jack shrugged and proceeded to the living room, picked up the evening paper that Charlotte always placed on his recliner for him, and sat to scan the news and sip his beer.

"Your dinner is cold." Charlotte started to make up a plate for Jack, clanking the mashed potato spoon onto the plate.

When she didn't hear an apology, she poked her head into the living room. Jack acted as if he hadn't heard her.

"Well? Do you want me to fix you a plate or not?"

"I'm not hungry. I grabbed a bite at the corner café earlier."

Charlotte huffed and stomped back into the kitchen. She shoveled his food into the trash, practically scraping the finish off the plate. The dish nearly shattered when she tossed it into the sink.

Jack didn't even bother to look up from his newspaper while Charlotte cleared the table as loudly as possible. But not a single stomp, clank, or crash seemed to bother him.

Still shaking, Charlotte lit a cigarette to calm herself. Her sliced finger throbbed. A part of her wished it had been her wrist.

Once she'd smoked half her cigarette and the nicotine began calming her nerves, Charlotte crushed the rest into the ashtray, marched to the living room, and perched her hands on her hips. She glared a hole through her husband's newspaper, waiting for him to notice. Hell, for him to even acknowledge her existence.

Jack casually turned the page and continued reading.

Charlotte stomped over and ripped the newspaper from his hands.

He gawked at her a moment, furrowing his brow. "What is your problem?"

"I'm married to an insensitive brute, that's my problem!"

"Excuse me?"

"There is no excuse! I spend hours slaving in the kitchen so you can have a hot meal waiting for you on the table when you get home, and you don't even have the decency to call to let me know you're going to be two hours late. And then you have the nerve to eat out when you knew I was making dinner at home."

Jack stood and headed for the door. "You know what? I've had a long, hard day. The last thing I need is to come home and get the third degree."

Charlotte was speechless.

"Maybe I shouldn't have come home," Jack said as he shoved open the screen door and walked out.

The door slammed behind him like a slap in the face. It took a moment for the shock to wear off enough for Charlotte to wipe the tears from her face and start after him.

Then she stopped. No. She wasn't going to chase him. If anyone was going to apologize, it should be Jack. She turned on her heel and headed back to the kitchen.

Charlotte filled the sink with soapy water and started in on the dishes. She banged the pots and plates as loudly as possible to ensure Jack heard her from the front porch.

Deep down, she yearned for her husband to slink back inside and slip his arms around her from behind. Then whisper an apology in her ear, swear his undying love and devotion, then spin her around and plant one of those long, passionate, movie kisses on her.

Apparently, that only happened on the big screen.

She finished washing and drying the dishes, listening for Jack. Not a sound.

Charlotte tried to calm her jitters with another cigarette. In the back of her mind, she heard Joan saying, "Did you hear about the Jeffersons? Bill ran off with his secretary."

She took a deep drag and exhaled a stream of smoke.

Jack's words came back to haunt her. "Maybe I shouldn't have come home."

Had Claire and Bill fought like this before he left for good?

You think you know people...

Charlotte finished her cigarette and retrieved a beer from the refrigerator. Stepping outside, she found Jack sitting on the porch, the orange glow from his cigarette illuminating his face.

She stood there a moment, hoping he would apologize. When he didn't, she extended the beer as a peace offering.

He took the beer but gave nothing in return. Not surprising, though. Hadn't their relationship been like that since their honeymoon? She gave. He took.

Jack took a drag on his cigarette and stared into the night.

When an apology didn't come, Charlotte relented and offered her own.

* * *

Charlotte buttered two slices of toast as her husband sat at the breakfast table, his face buried in the morning paper. She placed the toast on top of a plate of steaming scrambled eggs and set it in front of him.

"Would you like me to make you a lunch?"

"I have a lunch meeting."

"That's the third time this week," she said, her voice more shrill than she intended.

"Is it?" He took a bite of toast and sipped his coffee before returning to the paper.

So many things she wanted to say to him. All of which would likely start another fight. Better just to swallow the words. And the pain.

She made a piece of toast for herself and poured a second cup of coffee. Just as she sat across from Jack, he checked his watch and grunted. He folded the paper and tossed it on the table. Abandoning the eggs she made him, Jack stuck a toast wedge in his mouth and headed for the door.

Like a lost dog, Charlotte followed him only to watch him don his hat, grab his briefcase, and open the door to leave.

She leaned in, hoping for a kiss that didn't come.

* * *

Charlotte turned to cleaning as therapy. Pushing the heavy-duty Hoover around always helped her work out her frustrations. As she vacuumed, her mind tried to sort out what happened to her marriage. Had she failed to show her husband enough affection? Could it just be work stress making Jack seem so distant? Or could there be something (*someone*) else?

She glanced at the liquor cabinet. Maybe a cocktail to take the edge off? That's what her father used to say. Although it didn't help his marriage. Or his liver. She decided to clean a different room to help her avoid the temptation. And what better room to clean than the bathroom? It was the perfect metaphor for the way she felt.

As she scrubbed the bathroom sink, she gazed up at her reflection in the medicine cabinet mirror. Charlotte was still in her thirties, with no wrinkles to speak of, although the absence of laugh lines could be more indicative of her marriage than her age and skincare regimen.

She opened the medicine cabinet and retrieved a prescription bottle. *Mother's little helper*, her mom used to call them. After a moment's consideration, she put it back. The last thing she needed was to become dependent on one more thing that was sure to let her down.

Grabbing a pair of rubber gloves, she set her mind and energy toward cleaning the shower and the toilet. They certainly weren't going to clean themselves. Plus, she desperately needed the distraction.

Once she finished the bathroom, Charlotte made herself a sandwich and sat down to watch her favorite soap opera. All work and no play, as they say.

Sadly, instead of providing a mindless diversion, it only reminded her of the soap opera she was currently living. Her heart sank seeing one of the female characters walk in on her husband in bed with another woman. Her throat tightened, tears blurring her vision.

The phone rang, and Charlotte jumped. Wiping her eyes, she shuffled to the kitchen.

"Can you believe it?" Joan shouted through the earpiece.

"I... I was just as shocked as you were."

"And just as she was about to tell Allen she's pregnant!"

Once Joan got on a roll talking about their soaps, Charlotte had difficulty getting a word in edgewise. Fortunately, the kitchen phone had a long cord that could stretch into the laundry room.

"Everyone told her not to marry that louse," Joan continued.

Charlotte's heart hurt just thinking about it. She began sorting the laundry. Might as well accomplish something while Joan had her tied up.

Charlotte started separating out the whites, a habit she'd observed for as long as she could remember. Probably because whites showed the dirt more, making her feel like they needed to be prioritized. Or maybe it was just a habit she'd picked up from her mother.

Joan continued to babble.

"Oh, I know." Charlotte contributed.

Picking up one of her husband's white dress shirts, Charlotte noticed something on the shoulder. Was that foundation? Probably just dirt. But Jack worked in an office. How would he get dirty sitting behind a desk?

She examined the collar for more clues. There, like a neon sign, a smear of bright red lipstick. The color whores wear.

The handset cradled between her shoulder and neck dropped and bounced off the linoleum. Before she could retrieve it, the spiral cord retracted, sending the receiver skittering across the floor toward the kitchen.

"Hello? Charlotte, are you still there?"

For a moment, Charlotte felt like she'd fallen down a well. Darkness closed in around her. She was sinking, flailing her arms, unable to catch her breath. Someone called to her from above. A lifeline...

"Charlotte? Hello?"

She finally snapped out of her daze and realized the voice was coming from the receiver lying on the kitchen floor. Charlotte scrambled to the kitchen and picked up the phone.

"Charlotte? Are you okay?"

In a choked whisper, she answered, "I'll call you back."

* * *

When Jack returned home from work, Charlotte was sitting and waiting for him, arms crossed. If looks could kill, he'd be on the floor staring at the ceiling. Oblivious, Jack hung up his hat and coat and proceeded to fix himself a scotch. He took a sip and turned before finally noticing her glare.

"What?" he asked.

"You know what!" She threw his shirt at him. It bounced off his chest and fell to the floor.

Jack rolled his eyes. "Not this again..."

"I cook for you, clean for you, do your laundry... and this is the thanks I get?" Her throat tightened, tears threatening like a dark storm cloud. "You promised me it wouldn't happen again!"

"You're never gonna let it go, are you?"

Charlotte stared at him, aghast. "Well, maybe if you could keep it in your pants, I wouldn't have a problem 'letting it go'!"

"Here it comes," Jack said, throwing up his hands. "All aboard the paranoid express."

"Paranoid?" Charlotte snatched up Jack's makeup-stained shirt and shook it in his face. "Does this look like I'm just paranoid!"

Jack leaned forward until his face was only inches away from hers. "You're just as crazy as your mother."

Charlotte slapped him. "How dare you!"

Jack responded with the back of his hand, knocking her off balance. The force of the blow whipped her head to the side, her hair falling across her face.

The shock took a moment to wear off. Fortunately, Charlotte's hair concealed the tears pouring down her cheeks. She bolted into the bathroom, locked herself in, and sobbed.

It took a moment to gather the courage and examine her face in the mirror. Her cheek was fiery red, the initial sting now growing feverish. How could she be so stupid to believe he had changed?

* * *

Every time Charlotte thought she'd pulled herself together, she began to sob again. She was determined not to leave the bathroom until she could keep it together. Jack didn't deserve the satisfaction of seeing her cry. Even if it meant staying in the bathroom all night.

She stared at her tear-streaked face in the mirror, barely recognizing the woman she'd become. What if *she* left Jack? Started over. Or was it too late? If she did, where would she go? How would she support herself? She regretted not finishing college, instead settling for an "M.R.S. Degree."

Charlotte climbed into the tub and hugged her knees to her chest. She eyed the razor resting on the ledge. It called to her, assuring her that there was always a way out.

* * *

A knock came on the bathroom door. "Go away!" Charlotte yelled.

"Charlotte?"

"I said, go away."

"Charlotte, this is Dr. Fields."

It had been years since she'd heard that name. That calm, professional voice. But it couldn't be. Was her mind playing tricks on her again, reaching for a coping mechanism? A life-line?

The mellow voice continued. "Jack called me. He's concerned about you. I'm concerned about you."

Charlotte climbed out of the tub and checked herself in the mirror. Black mascara tears stained her cheeks.

"I'd like to help you, Charlotte," the doctor said. "But it would be much easier without this barrier between us."

Charlotte wet a washcloth and wiped her face.

"I... just... just give me a minute."

After towel-drying her cheeks, she powdered her face and ran a brush through her hair.

When Charlotte opened the door, Dr. Fields stood there smiling. He invited her to join him in the living room for a little chat. Charlotte seethed seeing Jack in his recliner, flipping through the magazine with Grace Kelly on the cover. Oh, how she craved a cigarette right now.

What had he told the doctor? *That she's crazy, just like her mother*. She shot a look at Jack, who returned a knowing grin. But as soon as Dr. Fields looked his way, Jack quickly transformed into the concerned husband.

"I'm sorry Jack called you all the way out here and wasted your valuable time."

The doctor leaned forward and steepled his fingers. "It's not a waste of time if it prevents you from having another nervous breakdown."

"Is... is that what you think?" She glanced at Jack, eyes shooting daggers, then back to the doctor. "Is that what he—"

"This isn't about Jack, right now," the doctor interrupted firmly before his voice mellowed into his thinly-veiled, condescending tone. "It's about what's best for you, Charlotte."

"How can this NOT be about Jack when he's the one having an affair?"

Jack denied the affair. Of Course.

Charlotte's blood boiled. "Really? Really!"

She glanced around for the makeup-stained shirt before locating it on top of the laundry pile. Charlotte marched her husband's shirt into the living room and presented the evidence to the doctor.

"Then what about this!"

Dr. Fields examined the shirt. "I'm afraid I don't see anything out of the ordinary..."

"Are you blind?" Charlotte snatched the shirt from him. "Can't you see..."

The foundation on the shoulder was gone.

The lipstick on the collar... vanished.

"I-I must have grabbed the wrong shirt."

Charlotte rushed back to the laundry room, checking each of his unwashed shirts. No sign of makeup on any of them. How could that be?

She wandered into the living room in a daze. Was it possible that she only saw what she expected to see?

"Well?" Jack asked.

Suddenly, it hit her. She had been in the bathroom for over an hour. Jack could've easily disposed of the evidence! She ran to the kitchen and looked in the trash.

No shirt.

As a matter of fact, the trashcan was empty. Was it empty before?

Charlotte rushed outside to the metal trashcans alongside the house. She yanked the lid off the first can and tossed it to the concrete with a loud clatter.

No shirt on top.

She tossed the lid off the other can. It was only half full. No shirt there, either. But...

He would've known she'd look for it. He must've buried it under some garbage, thinking she wouldn't go digging through the stinking waste.

Charlotte tipped over the can and began sifting through the refuse, searching for the smoking gun.

Drawn by the clatter of the trashcans, Jack and Dr. Fields ventured outside.

"Charlotte, what the hell are you doing?" Jack said.

"Don't you see, Dr. Fields? While I was in the bathroom crying my eyes out, he disposed of the evidence!"

Her confidence waned as she dug through the garbage without finding the shirt. Finally, she picked up the can and dumped the last of its contents onto the ground, digging through it with her bare hands.

It wasn't there.

Confused, Charlotte looked up at Dr. Fields, pleading with her eyes. "But... but it has to be here..."

"Charlotte," Dr. Fields said in a calming tone. "Why don't you come inside and get cleaned up so we can talk this over."

"You don't understand... I—I know what I saw."

The doctor smiled. "I don't doubt what you *believe* you saw..."

"You think I imagined it?"

"Now, Charlotte, I didn't say—"

"Do you think I'm crazy?"

"Please," Dr. Fields said, "come inside."

Dazed and bewildered, Charlotte staggered toward the house. Was it possible that she imagined everything? Dr. Fields placed his hand on her back and gently guided her back into the house.

* * *

"Here, I'd like you to take these," Dr. Fields said. "It'll help you relax."

Charlotte sat up in bed and palmed the pills.

Jack entered the room with a glass of water he'd filled from the kitchen tap. She took the glass and stared at the pills in her hand, then glanced up at the men. It was two against one. A fight she knew she couldn't win. Charlotte sighed and swallowed one bitter pill at a time.

Slipping under the covers, Charlotte lay back and closed her eyes. Who knows, with any luck, once the tranquilizers took her away to dreamland, she might find a loving, faithful husband there.

* * *

Jack walked Dr. Fields to the door. "Thanks for coming on such short notice, Oscar."

"What are old friends for?"

"Sigma Phi!" Jack said with a grin.

"Sigmund Freud!" Oscar replied with a laugh.

Jack closed and locked the door. His smile turned to a scowl as he glanced toward the bedroom.

* * *

As the days and weeks passed, Charlotte slept more and more. Cleaned less and less. Dinners became simpler, easy-to-make recipes. No sense spending hours preparing a meal that may end up back in the refrigerator or dumped in the trash on nights Jack came home late. Those nights became progressively more frequent.

After weeks of sinking deeper and deeper into depression, Charlotte was lucky to get out of bed by noon. The carpet hadn't been vacuumed or the kitchen floor mopped since... she couldn't remember when. This morning, she didn't even make the bed.

The only spark of joy left in her days was her soaps. Plural. She used to watch only one soap opera while eating her lunch, but now she was addicted to three. Was it because of the romantic interludes of lovers with their passion still aflame? Or the comfort in seeing others with lives more disastrous than hers?

She felt numb. Could it be the tranquilizers Dr. Fields prescribed? Or the result of a marital flame that had dwindled to a flickering candle, starved of oxygen?

Charlotte slogged into the kitchen and poured herself a cup of coffee. Black and bitter like her life. *You are what you drink, right?*

The toaster popped up a piece of toast nearly as black as the coffee. Charlotte considered scraping the excess char off and softening one side with butter, but... what was the point?

Shuffling into the living room, Charlotte set her cup and plate of toast on the coffee table before turning on the television and turning the dial to the first soap of the day.

As the picture tube heated up, she plopped down on the couch. Her robe fell open, exposing her thighs. A far-away memory bubbled to the surface of when she and Jack were first married and how a wardrobe slip like this would've prompted him to take her right there on the couch. Now, she was lucky if he noticed her at all.

Charlotte took a bite of the dry toast and washed it down with a mouthful of hot, bitter coffee. The signature organ music of *Search for Tomorrow* began as the title displayed amongst rolling clouds. The black and white screen made the ostensibly blue sky appear black. The perfect setting for her gloomy mood.

The phone rang, startling her. She let it ring a few more times, fearing it might be her mother in Brooklyn. Charlotte really didn't have the energy to put on a happy face for her. *Yes, Mom, everything's fine.* But mother would somehow know that things weren't fine by some tell in her voice. Then she'd have to spend ten minutes trying to convince her mother that everything was fine. And no, she hadn't produced any grandchildren since their last call.

But what if it was Jack? What if he was calling to tell her that he'd been a fool and that she should get gussied up so he could take her out for dinner tonight at a nice sit-down restaurant, maybe enjoy a couple cocktails, then go dancing before returning home and... no. The only way that would happen was if she could step through the television screen and into one of her soap operas.

The telephone continued its piercing ring. Why didn't they give up already? Just when she leaned forward to get up to answer... it stopped.

Thank God.

When the show went to commercial, the phone rang again. Two calls back-to-back? What were the odds? Did that mean the call was urgent? Charlotte sighed, set her cup down, then shuffled to the kitchen and picked it up on the seventh ring.

It was Joan.

"Are you okay?" Joan asked.

"I'm fine." Charlotte's tone belied her words.

"That's it. Get dressed," Joan said. "I'm taking you out to lunch."

Charlotte tried to object, but Joan refused to take no for an answer. And Charlotte didn't have the energy to argue.

After she hung up, Charlotte realized she would have to muster up the energy to get dressed and do her makeup.

She sighed.

Part of her wanted to go back to bed and dream of a happier life. But a distant part buried deep inside cried out, *Go. Get dressed up. Show the world you're not the crazy hausfrau your husband claims.*

An image flashed in Charlotte's mind of her out on the town in her housecoat, slippers, and hair pulled up in big, pink curlers like something from an *I Love Lucy* episode. That distant voice grew louder, bolder, crying out, *NO! Stop wallowing in misery. Put on a party dress, heels, and evening makeup like when you were young and carefree, like when you and Joan used to paint the town red. Like back in the good old days. Before Jack.*

It seemed like a lifetime ago. Another person ago.

A surge of excitement bubbled in her bosom. A feeling she hadn't felt in... she couldn't remember how long. A feeling buried so deep she assumed it dead.

Charlotte was like a forgotten damsel locked in a dungeon for years, deep inside the earth where no one could hear her pleas to escape. She took a deep breath, exhaled, and set the old Charlotte free.

* * *

The doorbell rang as Charlotte finished applying the deep red lipstick she'd unearthed from the bottom of her makeup bag. She tried to remember when she'd last worn it. Charlotte used to fix her face and apply lipstick every night before Jack came home from work. At least until she found out about his first affair. Before the nervous breakdown.

After she was released from the hospital, Charlotte refused to wear makeup. She wanted her husband to see how ugly she felt on the inside. But that was short-lived. He didn't get the hint. Like men ever get hints unless they are of the *I want to make love* variety. Even then, it wasn't a given.

Soon, she realized that not wearing makeup was counterproductive. If her husband had been tempted by a woman younger and prettier than her, how would not wearing makeup inspire him to limit himself to home cooking?

That later led her to put all her efforts into making herself as attractive as possible. It even worked for a while as they started making love more often. But, like all things, everything eventually returned to *normal*. She suspected that Jack had strayed again, once or twice, but convinced herself it was just her imagination. Or was it her brain's own self-defense mechanism trying to keep her from going insa—

The doorbell rang again.

When Charlotte opened the door, Joan's jaw dropped. Then she smiled. "I'm sorry, I must have the wrong house. I'm looking for a mousey little housewife with no self-esteem."

Charlotte blushed. *Wow*. When was the last time she did that? The warmth of her cheeks felt good. The smile felt good. Hell, it was nice to feel anything again.

"Don't just stand there, Cinderella," Joan said. "Let's go have a ball!"

* * *

Charlotte rolled down her passenger-side window enough to enjoy some fresh air but careful not to muss her hairdo. The afternoon sun felt good on her skin. She wondered if this was how a tulip felt in the spring when its first shoot broke through the earth after a long winter buried in the deep, dark soil.

They talked while Joan drove, starting with the weather. Then Joan filled her in on the latest neighborhood gossip. Then there was the recipe Joan found in the latest Good Housekeeping magazine that Charlotte just had to try.

Eventually, Joan artfully danced around the subject, trying to unearth the cause of Charlotte's recent spiral into depression without actually coming out and asking. Careful not to pick the emotional scab enough to make it bleed.

Charlotte deftly changed the subject, parrying each prodding for more information until her friend surrendered her investigation without too much fight. She knew Joan would likely wait until Charlotte had eaten her lunch and let her guard down before trying again. Who knows, by then, Charlotte may finally be ready to bare her soul.

They parked on the street about half a block from the restaurant. It had been so long since Charlotte had been out of the house, let alone worn heels; she felt like a newborn foal attempting to walk for the first time. If she wasn't careful, she was liable to roll an ankle.

But what was the rush anyway? Slow down. Enjoy being out of the house. Midnight would come soon enough, Cinderella.

Charlotte slowed as she caught her reflection in a store window. Was that really her? She stopped and glanced over her shoulder to see if maybe she had glimpsed another woman. A prettier one. One who hadn't stopped caring and *let herself go*, as Jack liked to say.

She smiled, and her reflection smiled back. The smile looked good on her.

Charlotte pretended to be window shopping as she studied her reflection. She turned sideways, examining her figure. Gravity hadn't taken *too* much of a toll. Her bullet bra kept her breasts looking as perky as when she was eighteen. Sure, she'd added a few pounds lately, but mostly in all the right places. Her hips, round and shapely, accentuated her hourglass figure. No one complained about Marilyn Monroe's shapely figure.

She certainly hadn't put on as much weight as the other neighborhood women whose bodies had been ravaged by childbirth. But if Charlotte had been able to have children, would that have created a stronger bond with her husband? Kept him from straying?

"Do you see something you like?" Joan asked.

"Uh... no, not really."

Just as she turned, she caught a shocking glimpse reflected in the storefront window. Was that Jack walking on the other side of the street? With another woman on his arm?

"Are you sure?" Joan asked. "We can go in if you like."

Charlotte started to shake. How could he? And right out in broad daylight?

"Charlotte? Are you okay?"

She spun and glared across the street at Jack and a young brunette, arm in arm, smiling, laughing. A bus passed, obscuring her view.

Charlotte waited. Squinted. She had to know for sure if it was him. The bus passed the couple, revealing beyond a shadow of a doubt that the man... wasn't Jack. Too tall. Too thin.

"Charlotte?"

"Sorry, I—I thought I saw someone I knew."

When they reached the restaurant, a gentleman held the door for them, tipping his hat to Charlotte with a smile.

"Thank you," Charlotte said, blushing. Jack used to open doors for her when they were courting. The last few years, on the rare occasions they went somewhere together, she had to open her own car door and hurry just to catch up to him.

The hostess sat them in a booth with springy, red vinyl seats and a traditional Italian red and white checkered tablecloth. It seemed like months since she and Jack had been out to a restaurant. When they were first married, they used to go out to eat every Sunday afternoon after Mass. A year after they said their vows, Jack stopped attending Mass except for Christmas and Easter. Before long, Charlotte followed suit. She got tired of having to explain her husband's whereabouts.

The waiter brought them menus and chilled water glasses. It felt wonderful to be served by someone else for a change.

The two friends continued making small talk. It mainly consisted of Joan bragging about her children. A boy and a girl. Her son was pitching in Little League. Her whip-smart daughter declared that she wanted to be a nurse when she grew up.

Charlotte scanned the menu. She wanted spaghetti but was afraid she'd get spots of marinara on her Sunday dress. Fettuccine Alfredo would be a safer choice. And a salad.

When she looked up from her menu, Charlotte noticed a man at a table smoking a cigarette and gazing at her. She reflexively looked down and then back to Joan. They talked some more, and when Charlotte glanced back, the man was still ogling her. He smiled and shot her a wink. Charlotte smiled back before shyly averting her eyes. What was she doing? He's going to think she's flirting with him!

The waiter returned to take their drink orders. When she glanced back at the man, he stood and tossed some bills on the table. She tried not to look directly at him, tracking him out of the corner of her eye. But as he neared her table, she couldn't resist looking up. He smiled and tipped his hat.

Joan smirked. "Are you blushing?"

"What? No!"

"You *are* blushing!"

Charlotte suppressed a smile and looked away, not wanting to give Joan any ammunition. She pretended to watch a waitress carrying an order to another table as if she were appraising the entrees on her tray. Across the restaurant, a businessman watched the waitress too, only he was appraising the waitress's hips as she sashayed past.

Charlotte recognized that look. She'd seen Jack do it a hundred times.

Their eyes met. Their jaws dropped. Jack?

She gasped and turned away.

When she looked back, the man held up a menu, obscuring his face. Charlotte's heart raced, her eyes burning a hole through the menu, waiting for him to lower it.

He didn't. Was he hiding? That's when she noticed the young blonde sitting across from him. Where did he find this floozy? The steno pool? Or was she his new secretary?

Her grip tightened on her fork.

"Charlotte?"

She felt herself rise like a marionette. But who was pulling her strings?

Joan grabbed her hand. "Charlotte? Are you okay?"

Her blood boiling, Charlotte leapt from her seat, clenching the fork hard enough to bend it, ready to stab it into Jack's cheating heart.

But as she reached the table, she collided with a waiter in a cacophony of silverware and china. The tray sailed through the air as plates full of food crashed around them. Her once spotless Sunday dress became a crime scene of marinara.

"Madame! I'm so sorry!" the waiter shouted in a thick Italian accent. "I did not see you!"

Mortified, Charlotte apologized profusely. She bent to help the waiter clean up the mess. As they attempted to shuttle fistfuls of pasta and shattered plates onto the tray, the manager rushed over, repeatedly apologizing for the clumsy waiter.

Tears streamed down Charlotte's face. "I'm so sorry. It was all my fault."

The manager clicked his fingers in the air, summoning a busboy to clean up the mess before returning to Charlotte. "We will, of course, reimburse you for your cleaning expenses," the manager said. "Again, my sincerest apologies."

Charlotte suddenly felt the weight of a restaurant full of glares. Her ears burned with whispers of pity and disdain. She desperately wanted to dig a hole and crawl into it.

Charlotte's eyes met Joan's. Her friend's pained expression made Charlotte feel even lower. Not only had she humiliated herself but her only friend as well. And all because of... *Jack*.

In all the commotion, she'd forgotten what caused this spectacle in the first place. The bell over the front door dinged as she eyed the booth where she'd seen Jack sitting with that other woman.

The booth was empty.

Charlotte glanced toward the door right as it closed. Was she imagining things, or did Jack and his mistress escape during all the commotion? Her mind reeled. Could Jack be right? Was she crazy like her mother?

She had to know.

Charlotte bolted for the door, breaking a heel in her haste and rolling her ankle. White-hot pain shot up her leg. She stumbled and fell to one knee, driving it into the floor. Charlotte cried out but refused assistance from an elderly man in a nearby booth.

She couldn't let Jack get away without knowing that she knew.

Removing her heels, Charlotte limped out the door and onto the sidewalk. She glanced left and right. Which way had they gone? Were they hiding among the other lunchtime pedestrians? Panic surged through her veins. She needed to confront them. But where had they gone?

There. Was that Jack's car pulling away from the curb? Charlotte galloped after the vehicle. If she could only get close enough to read the license plate to confirm that she wasn't crazy. But every step on her rolled ankle was like being stabbed with a knife. And where did all these people come from? *Get out of the way*!

Then her ankle buckled, and she hit the ground, the sidewalk digging into her knees and palms. *No! They're getting away*! She clambered to her feet as the traffic light up ahead turned green, and the vehicle sped off.

Despondent, Charlotte grabbed fistfuls of hair in frustration, a scream rising inside her, ready to blow like a steam whistle. Then she caught her reflection in a store window. Black tears streaked her face, her red lips twisted in a grotesque, clown-like grimace. Her best Sunday dress appeared blood-spattered from the collision with the waiter, her battered knees protruding from her torn nylons.

Horrified at the sight of herself, Charlotte's pent-up scream evaporated. Maybe Jack was right. After all, what did this pathetic scarecrow have to offer a man like him?

* * *

Jack came home to find "You're Cheatin' Heart" by Hank Williams Jr. on the phonograph, playing on repeat, shattered vinyl strewn across the living room floor. Black marks marred the wall where the records had struck. Empty album covers of Sinatra, Nat King Cole, and The Platters lay scattered across the carpet.

Charlotte lay passed out in her chair, a half-empty decanter of Scotch and an uncapped prescription bottle resting on the coffee table. Her hand still clutched the drained whiskey glass in her lap.

Jack could feel the heat percolating up into his face, causing his temples to throb. That yodeling fool on the phonograph was about to drive him mad!

Jack rushed to the turntable and dragged the needle across the record, grinding the song to a halt. Then he turned his attention to Charlotte.

He wanted to grab his wife and shake her, snap her out of whatever manic-depressive state she'd gotten herself into again. But then he noticed the open prescription bottle. How many had she taken? And when?

Was she still breathing? He watched for a moment. Charlotte's chest appeared to rise and fall ever so slightly, her breathing shallow but steady.

Jack took a step back until his anger receded. He needed some time to assess the situation. To think all this through.

Avoiding the vinyl shrapnel on the floor, Jack retrieved a whiskey glass for himself and poured two fingers. He navigated back through the musical minefield and sat across from Charlotte.

And watched.

And listened to her shallow breathing. Wondering if each would be her last.

Casually retrieving a cigarette pack from his sportcoat, Jack tapped one out and lit it. He inhaled deeply and released the smoke through his nostrils. Yes, this situation required careful deliberation.

* * *

An hour passed.

Then two.

Jack watched her subtle breathing. In. And out.

But it never ceased.

He considered his options.

Apparently, however many pills his wife had taken hadn't been a lethal dose.

Jack ran the cost/benefit analysis over in his head one last time, then sighed. He strolled over to the phone and spun the rotary dial, pausing on the final number. He glanced back at the living room one last time, then dialed the last digit.

The phone rang on the other end.

After three rings, a woman answered.

"Hi Patty, this is Jack. Sorry to disturb you at this hour, but is Oscar there?"

After a moment, Dr. Fields came to the phone.

"Sorry to interrupt your evening, Oscar. But I need a favor."

* * *

Charlotte awoke. Groggy. Confused. She tried to open her eyes, but the bright morning sunlight was blinding. Her head ached, and her stomach groaned. She hadn't felt hungover like this since college.

Opening her eyes a slit, Charlotte let them adjust until she could gradually open them enough to get her bearings. She was surrounded by white. For a brief moment, she thought she might've died and gone to heaven. But her stomach cramps and pounding headache suggested the opposite.

As the room swam into focus, she realized it wasn't quite as white as she first thought. It was... off-white. Was she in a hospital room? Had she been in an accident? She searched her memory but couldn't find it through the fog.

Charlotte reached to massage her temple, but her wrist seemed caught on something. It must be tangled in her covers. She tried to free herself, but her other hand was also constrained. Frustration built as she tugged at the covers, unable to free herself. The harder she struggled, the more she panicked, struggling and thrashing until the covers finally fell away, revealing thick leather straps buckled around her wrists, securing her arms to metal bed rails.

What kind of place was this? She glanced around for clues and noticed the bars on the window. Why would a hospital have bars on the windows? Who would want to break into a hospital?

Charlotte racked her brain as to how she could've ended up here. Images flashed in her mind: admiring herself in a store window, clad in her Sunday finest, her hair done up. Then, flashes of another reflection, her hair frazzled, nylons ripped where her mangled knees protruded, her favorite dress ruined (*was that blood spattered all over her dress?*). Had she been struck on the head and mugged?

Charlotte cried out. How long had she been here, and how long before she could get out?

"Nurse! Nurse!" She frantically yanked on her restraints. "Nurse! Anybody!"

Suddenly, the doorknob rattled, accompanied by a jingle of keys. A stocky matron entered with a dour expression. "What's all the fuss about?"

A barrage of questions poured out, along with a fountain of tears. "Where am I? Why am I here? And why am I restrained like some kind of criminal?"

The image of her crimson-spattered reflection flashed in her mind again. Was she a criminal? Had she committed bloody murder?

"You're at Eloise State Hospital," the nurse said, retrieving a clipboard attached to the foot of her bed.

"Eloise?" Charlotte gasped. "The crazy farm?"

The nurse scowled. "We do NOT use that vulgar term here."

"But... but why?" Her mind rewound like a reel-to-reel player to Jack slapping her. Then, her blood-drenched reflection. Could she have—

"W—where's my husband?"

Oh, God! Had she finally snapped and killed Jack?

The nurse looked up from the clipboard. "It appears your husband brought you here. Apparently, you tried—"

To kill him?

"—to take your life."

"But I don't..."

The nurse flipped the page of her chart. Her eyebrow raised. "Hmm. Apparently, this isn't your first visit to Eloise."

"What? No. That was—I just had a nervous breakdown." *What was this nurse implying?* "I had a miscarriage, and my husband and I were having problems and—"

The nurse looked down her nose at Charlotte with a subtle smirk.

"I'm NOT crazy!"

The nurse's smirk broadened. "Let's leave the diagnoses to the doctor, shall we?" She made a note on the clipboard before letting it drop. It swung on its chain and the metal clipboard clanged against the bed rails. The matron turned heel and headed toward the door.

"Wait!" Charlotte cried, wrestling against the leather bands securing her wrists. "What about these?"

"Once the doctor determines that you're no longer a risk to yourself or others, we'll see about removing your restraints."

"No! Please! You can't leave me like this!"

The nurse raised her eyebrows as if to say, *See? These types of outbursts are why you are shackled to your bed.*

When the nurse turned again to leave, Charlotte pleaded with her to at least give her a drink of water. The nurse sighed, then went to the bathroom sink, filled a paper cup half full from the tap, and brought it to her. The tepid water tasted metallic and had a strange odor, but her mouth was so dry she would've drank anything.

"The doctor will be by later."

With that, the nurse left. The metal door slammed with the finality of a prison cell.

* * *

Charlotte tried to sleep, hoping it would make the time pass quicker until the doctor arrived and she could plead her case. But her mind kept searching for the lost moments before she awoke at the state hospital. She came up blank.

Charlotte listened to the seconds tick away on the wall clock, which, like the windows, was secured with metal bars.

Footfalls echoed down the hallway. She tried her best to sit up and look "normal" in case it was the doctor. But the footfalls continued down the hall and faded away.

A man screamed somewhere nearby. Chills skittered up her spine like a legion of spiders. Charlotte had never heard a grown man scream like that. What did it take to provoke such terror?

She wanted desperately to cover her ears and silence the man's tortured cries, but her restraints left her helpless against the assault.

Footsteps rushed down the hall past her room. Moments later, the man's screams abruptly stopped.

Charlotte trembled like a child. Is this what she had to look forward to? Tears soaked her cheeks, but she was powerless to whisk them away. She wanted to call out, but if the staff heard her cries echoing through the halls, would they silence her, too?

Charlotte wept quietly until she ran out of tears. And finally surrendering to sleep.

* * *

Charlotte's bladder felt like it was about to burst. She attempted to sit up, but the restraints held fast. What if no one came back to check on her until morning?

She tried convincing herself that this was only a nightmare and that any minute, she would awaken in her own bed with Jack lying beside her.

The pain from the pressure was too much to bear. Charlotte closed her eyes and resigned herself to the fact that she would wet the bed when footsteps echoed toward her room. *Please let it be a nurse!*

Keys jingled outside the door.

"Hello? Hello?" Charlotte called.

The door opened, and Dr. Fields walked in. Her heart leaped in her chest. "Dr. Fields! You don't know how glad I am to see you!"

The stodgy nurse tromped in behind him. Without a word, the doctor donned his reading glasses and examined her chart. Any thought of this possibly being a social call evaporated. Was he just making routine rounds and failed to notice it was Charlotte?

"Oscar, it's me. Jack's wife, Char—"

Nurse Stodgy shoved a thermometer under Charlotte's tongue, cutting her off. She monitored her watch without bothering to look up.

Dr. Fields lowered his reading glasses and looked her up and down. "So it is." He glanced at his wristwatch and scribbled something on her chart.

"This is all very confusing," Charlotte said around the thermometer.

Nurse Stodgy forced Charlotte's jaw shut and gave her a scowl.

"Mmhmm." The doctor scribbled some more. "I imagine it is."

Fields studied Charlotte for a moment. Was he waiting for her to say something? She didn't want to open her mouth again and incur the wrath of Nurse Stodgy.

Finally, the nurse removed the thermometer and verified the reading before giving it a shake. "98.5."

Dr. Fields jotted it down as Nurse Stodgy placed the blood pressure cuff around Charlotte's arm.

"Do you know why you're here?" he asked.

"I'm afraid I don't."

He scribbled on the chart.

Charlotte's heart sank. Was that the wrong answer? She didn't want to give them any reason to keep her here in this horrible place a minute longer.

"What's the last thing you remember?"

Charlotte's crimson-stained reflection flashed in her mind. "I..." She closed her eyes and shook the horrifying image away. What *was* the last thing she remembered? Suddenly, a lifeline.

"I remember my friend Joan taking me to lunch..."

"Mmhmm." The doctor nodded.

The nurse finished taking her blood pressure and gave the reading to the doctor to record.

"Anything else?" he asked.

Charlotte's bladder ached so bad she could barely think. She finally asked to be allowed to relieve herself. Fields studied her for a moment as if gauging whether she was merely trying to escape interrogation. He finally relented and nodded to the nurse.

The matron loosened Charlotte's arm and leg restraints. It felt so good to be freed. If she ever got out of this place, she vowed never to take her liberty for granted again.

After being escorted into the closet-sized bathroom, Charlotte pulled the doorknob until the door stopped abruptly on Nurse Stodgy's foot. It took her a moment to realize that it was no accident. Were they afraid she would lock herself in? She glanced at the doorknob and noticed it didn't have a lock. Was she that far gone that she couldn't be trusted to be out of their sight unless restrained?

It was bad enough to take away her liberty, but now they were even denying her basic privacy. Any last shred of dignity she may have had left was now gone.

Charlotte self-consciously lifted her thin cotton gown and noticed that they hadn't even afforded her any underwear.

After a seeming eternity emptying her bladder, Charlotte washed her hands. She caught her dull reflection in the polished steel mirror and stifled a sob. The hair she had worked so hard to style for her lunch date with Joan now hung in unkempt, oily tendrils.

Keep it together, Charlotte. The calmer you stay, the sooner they'll see that there is no reason to keep you here.

She briefly finger-combed her hair and put on a brave face before returning to the bed.

Nurse Stodgy gripped Charlotte's wrist and reached for the strap.

"Is this really necessary?" Charlotte asked, her voice sounding shriller than expected. "It's not like I could escape, locked in here with bars on the windows."

The nurse's grip tightened. "This is for your own good."

Charlotte offered the doctor a pleading look.

He said, "Once you've been evaluated and deemed no longer a threat to yourself... or others, you'll be allowed to—"

Go home?

"...join the others."

Join the others?

"No, please! I just want to go home! I'm fine now, really!"

Charlotte howled as the nurse cinched the strap so tight it nearly cut off her circulation.

She pleaded with Dr. Fields as the nurse continued to secure her wrists and ankles to the bed. *This can't be happening!*

"I think that's enough for today," the doctor said. He scribbled something on a small pad, tore off the sheet, and handed it to the nurse. "Be sure she gets these every eight hours."

As the nurse exited, Charlotte pled with Dr. Fields. "Please... I promise I'll be good! I swear!"

Doctor Fields strolled around to her bedside, smiled, and then leaned in close to whisper in Charlotte's ear, "Jack sends his regards."

* * *

Charlotte sobbed for nearly twenty minutes before Nurse Stodgy returned with pills and a Dixie cup filled with tap water. Charlotte tried to appeal to the nurse's compassionate side to finally remove her restraints so she could wipe away the tears and snot streaming down her face. "But what if I have to go to the bathroom again?"

The nurse leaned over, and for a fleeting moment, Charlotte gained a glimmer of hope that she might show some compassion and un-buckle her restraints. Instead, the nurse re-trieved a metal bedpan from under the bed, hiked up Charlotte's gown, and shoved the ice-cold bedpan under Charlotte's naked rear. Apparently, this nurse didn't have a *compassionate side*.

Before long, the medication kicked in, and Charlotte drifted off into a tempest of ghastly nightmares. Every couple of hours, she would surface from the dizzying haze only to sink back down soon after.

Charlotte awakened to a nurse checking her bedpan. What time was it? Hell, what day was it? The nurse squeezed Charlotte's cheeks and yanked open her jaw to administer another dose of meds. Charlotte dutifully choked them down with the little water afforded by the paper cup shoved in her mouth.

She hated the foggy, dizzying feeling of the medication. Still, it did help break up the interminable monotony of being strapped to the bedrails with mattress springs and a metal bedpan digging into your flesh.

* * *

The hours became days, and the days became a week. By now, Charlotte had no more tears and only a sliver of hope. She'd become comfortably numb.

Keys jingled in the hall, and Nurse Stodgy burst through the door. "All right, Sleeping Beauty, it's time to get you up and moving."

If only a prince would come and save her with a kiss. Her heart ached at the realization that her once charming prince hadn't even visited her once since she'd been here, as far as she knew. Or was she being too hard on him? Could he have visited while she was in a medicated stupor? At this point, Charlotte wasn't even sure how long she'd been at Eloise.

The nurse mechanically unbuckled Charlotte's restraints without concern for how the stiff leather straps had cut into her flesh. As soon as they were removed, Charlotte rubbed the wounds on her wrists and ankles, praying the scars wouldn't be permanent. Despite her stiff muscles and the raw pain from the restraints, it felt wonderful to no longer be confined to a hospital bed. She felt like a prisoner finally freed and couldn't wait to sleep in her own bed again.

Nurse Stodgy crossed her arms. "Let's go, we don't have all day!"

Charlotte sat up and swung her legs over the side of the bed. Her head swam, and her whole body felt stiff. She waited a moment for her head to clear. Once the nurse's impatient scowl swirled back into focus, Charlotte attempted to stand. Her legs felt weak and unsteady. The dizzying medication made her sway like a drunken sailor.

"Follow me," Nurse Stodgy said, heading for the door.

Charlotte followed her into the hallway, struggling to keep up with the stocky matron. It was like she was learning to walk again. But where was the nurse taking her? Was she finally getting released?

Weeping sounds came from one of the rooms they passed. Was that what she sounded like?

Farther down the hallway, a woman hummed a singsong tune over and over, like a little child.

"Mommy!" a man shouted, startling Charlotte. "Mommy!" Behind one of the doors, the man's shouting degraded into a pathetic mantra of "Mommy, no... mommy, no..."

At the end of the hall, the nurse led Charlotte into a large, open shower area. At least she was given a chance to clean up a bit before being released. Nothing would feel better after a week (*was it a week?*) in bed than a nice, hot shower.

The nurse handed Charlotte a thin, too-small towel and a half-used bar of soap with black pubic hair embedded in it.

Nurse Stodgy glanced at her watch. "You've got five minutes."

Charlotte turned her back to the nurse as she disrobed, trying to maintain some shred of dignity. She had never felt so vulnerable in her life.

The metal shower handle screeched as Charlotte turned it on. A blast of freezing water stole her breath. Jumping back, she nearly lost her footing on the slippery tile floor.

Charlotte tested the water with her hand, waiting for it to warm.

"Three minutes!" the nurse shouted.

Charlotte flinched. There was no time to wait for warm water. She braced herself and plunged into the frigid stream, briskly rubbing the soap over her shuddering body as quickly as possible. She winced as the soapy water stung the wounds on her wrists and ankles.

"Two minutes!" the nurse announced, staring at her wristwatch.

Charlotte considered asking for shampoo and conditioner but realized the futility of it.

She bar-soap-lathered her hair as best she could, sensing the nurse's watch counting down until—

"One minute!"

The water was just beginning to reach room temperature when the nurse finally yelled, "Times up!"

The shower handle shrieked as the nurse cut off the flow. Charlotte turned, covering her breasts with one arm and her privates with her other hand. Nurse Stodgy held Charlotte's towel just out of reach and smirked as if relishing her humiliation. After watching Charlotte shiver a moment, the nurse tossed Charlotte the towel, forcing her to momentarily uncover herself to catch it.

The threadbare towel barely had enough fiber left to dry herself with. Once Charlotte dried off the best she could, the nurse gave her a thin white gown. Charlotte stared at the nurse for a moment, hoping she might produce a pair of panties and a bra.

"Well?" the nurse said.

Still shivering, Charlotte turned her back to the nurse and slipped the gown over her head. The gown was obviously a temporary covering to get her back to her room, where she could get dressed in the clothes she'd worn here. Charlotte searched her memory again of the night she was admitted. Had she packed an extra set of clothes? At least some clean undergarments?

As they exited the shower area, Nurse Stodgy turned right, just as Charlotte attempted to head left toward her room.

"Where do you think you're going?" the nurse asked brusquely.

Charlotte's head was still cloudy, but she was pretty sure her room was the opposite way the nurse was leading her.

"I thought we were going back to my room."

"*Your room*?" the nurse laughed. "Where do you think you are, The Grand Hotel?"

Charlotte gawked at the nurse, dumbfounded. "But I need to get dressed."

Nurse Stodgy let out a hearty laugh. "What were you expecting, Cinderella, a ball gown?"

As Nurse Leslie approached, she covered her mouth to stifle a laugh.

"Well," Charlotte said defiantly, "I'm not driving home in this flimsy thing."

The smile dissipated from Nurse Stodgy's face. "Who said anything about going home?"

The realization hit Charlotte like a wrecking ball. Was that true? Were they really planning on keeping her here? And for how long? Almost as if to answer her question, a wrinkled, old hag meandered by in a similar cotton gown and flashed a toothless smile.

Charlotte had to force herself not to scream. What if she never got out of this madhouse? She suddenly felt numb all over.

As Nurse Leslie passed, Nurse Stodgy called out to her.

The young nurse stopped and turned back, the smile on her face turning to fear. "Yes, ma'am?"

"Nurse Leslie, please show Mrs. Davis to the common area. And make sure she is acquainted with the house rules."

"Yes, ma'am. Right away, ma'am."

Nurse Leslie took Charlotte by the arm and guided her down the hall. Charlotte was still in shock, her mind blank.

"Oh, and Mrs. Davis?" Nurse Stodgy called out.

Hearing her name, Charlotte stopped and turned.

Nurse Stodgy smiled. "Welcome to Eloise."

* * *

Nurse Leslie led Charlotte into the common area. The large, open room contained a couple dozen patients milling about to the soundtrack of department store Muzak. One group sat in wooden chairs before a snowy black-and-white television screen mounted high on the wall. Others sat at tables playing cards or checkers. The rest either wandered aimlessly about the room or had staked out a spot against the wall.

One woman meandered about the room, bending over to pick up imaginary breadcrumbs from the floor. Charlotte wondered if this tortured soul was trying to find her way home. What Charlotte wouldn't give to go home again.

A young woman with frazzled hair sat curled in a corner, rocking and whispering. She periodically glanced over at an imaginary confidant but never made consistent eye contact.

Nurse Leslie rattled off a quick rundown of the rules. "Lunch is at noon, dinner at five, meds as scheduled, lights out at ten. Do what the staff tells you, and you won't have any trouble. Understand?"

Charlotte nodded and watched with relief as Nurse Leslie headed to the nurse's station and joined the rest of the staff behind the large glass window, where they smoked and kept a casual eye on the patients.

Her relief quickly evaporated once she realized she was now on her own... in a room full of mental patients.

Charlotte suddenly felt as exposed as she did in the showers.

Frozen, she surveyed the room, her senses on high alert.

Then came that feeling every woman knows. Call it female intuition or just an inbred instinct for survival — the feeling that someone was behind her. Staring. Close enough to—

Charlotte spun and came face-to-face with a lanky, pale, red-headed man with wide eyes and a nicotine-stained grin.

"Hi, I'm Danny. You're new here. What are you in for?"

Charlotte backed away. "I—I don't really know."

"Yeah, me neither." He released a shrill laugh. "I'm not crazy, though."

Do crazy people know they're crazy? Charlotte wondered.

She glimpsed movement out of the corner of her eye — an odd-looking figure angling in her direction. Charlotte turned to gauge their intentions, and the sight stole her breath. It was a man with a severe cleft palate shuffling toward her. He looked like someone had swung an ax and buried it in the middle of his face, nearly splitting it in two, leaving a gaping fleshy gutter bisecting his face. As he passed, the two-faced man tried to smile. At least, she thought it was a smile. She must've made a face because Danny placed a hand on her shoulder.

Charlotte jerked away.

"Don't worry about him. He looks like hell, but he's harmless. I'm harmless, too!" Danny scratched his head. When he did, his sleeve revealed railroad-track scars on the inside of his wrist.

Noticing her gaze, he pulled down his sleeve. "Well, harmless to others, anyway."

Danny rubbed the straight-razor scars and gazed at his feet.

Charlotte looked away, a lump developing in her throat.

Assessing the people around her, Charlotte didn't think they looked much different than people you might see at the park, except for the fact they were all wearing pajamas.

But on closer inspection, something seemed a bit off with each of them: the slack jaw and faraway stare, the man whose eyes traced the path of an invisible fly, and the black-haired woman who seemed to be washing her hands over and over again.

A middle-aged woman in a rocking chair rocked an invisible baby.

The one that disturbed her the most was a wheelchair-bound man with thick eyebrows and a receding hairline whose eyes stared, unblinking, drool leaking from the corner of his mouth, his expression a blank slate.

"We're all harmless, you know," Danny said, breaking the silence. "Except for that one."

He pointed out the sullen man in the wheelchair. Danny rolled up his other sleeve and showed her a ragged purple wound that looked like someone had taken a bite out of his forearm and then sewed the mouthful of flesh back on. The skin around the wound faded into a sickly yellow.

Charlotte's skin crawled.

"He's a biter," Danny said. "At least he was. Before they gave him the pick."

"The pick?"

"Yeah. That's where they take this long, icepick-like tool and shove it into your eye socket, all the way into your brain." Danny mimicked the movements as if he were performing the procedure himself. "Then they jiggle it around until click! Out goes the lights."

He tapped his temple, his eyes wide. "It's like the party's over and... and all that's left is the empty beer cans scattered on the floor."

Charlotte stole a tentative peek at the wheelchair-bound man that Danny called *The Biter*. He sure seemed harmless now.

A female patient whirled and gamboled about the room, catching Charlotte's eye. The thin, sprightly creature didn't seem to have a care in the world. In a strange way, Charlotte envied her.

As the demented dancer angled toward The Biter, Charlotte's chest tightened. She glanced back and forth between the two. The man didn't seem aware of her whirling toward him. He didn't seem aware of anything.

The closer the lady sashayed toward him, the more anxious Charlotte became. The dancer seemed oblivious to the threat she was heading toward. Charlotte held her breath as the lady spun and waltzed straight toward The Biter. Just as she reached the wheelchair, Charlotte gasped.

The dancer suddenly pirouetted in front of the wheelchair, then leaped away, avoiding the catatonic man at the last second, just as The Biter's jaw snapped shut.

Charlotte released her pent-up breath. Was that just a reflex? Or was The Biter like a crocodile lying in wait for its prey to swim by? Could there be some primal instinct deep inside his brain that the lobotomy hadn't destroyed, awaiting an opportunity to strike?

Despite Danny's reassurances, she knew these patients couldn't *all* be harmless. She needed to stay alert if she had any hope of getting out of here in one piece.

* * *

Danny followed Charlotte around the rest of the day like a lost puppy. So far, he had not only proved to be harmless but helpful. Danny knew all the routines and who to avoid — both patients and staff. He even shared his cigarettes.

Lunch and dinner were served in the cafeteria. The food was surprisingly good. They made fresh bread on the premises every day. At lunch, there was ginger cake for dessert, and at dinner, they had pie, both made in their own bakery.

Charlotte's anxiety level decreased as the day wore on. And why not? She was getting three square meals she didn't have to prepare, cigarettes, and those magic pills they dispensed three times a day. Things could definitely be worse. She'd even made a friend.

The strange behavior and bizarre quirks the other patients exhibited had gone from terrifying aberrations to curious tics. In some, like the woman coddling her imaginary baby, even an endearment.

But she still feared turning her back on any of them.

As the sun set outside the barred windows and the shadows stretched across the courtyard, she noticed the patients becoming increasingly agitated.

The invisible fly tracker appeared to be tracking a swarm.

The mother rocking her imaginary baby rocked faster and faster.

The hand washer turned to hand wringing.

And The Biter began snapping at *everyone*.

Even Danny became increasingly fidgety.

Charlotte reminded herself not to let her guard down. Not even for an instant.

Suddenly, the Muzak stopped.

And so did everyone around her.

What did that mean? Was this some kind of twisted version of musical chairs where the last one standing had to sleep on the floor?

The night shift nurses filed out of their glass bunker, joined by several orderlies.

The head night shift nurse, Nurse Ratcliff, called for the patients to form an orderly line for the dispensing of the meds. Danny called her *Nurse Ratface* because of her pinched face and beady eyes.

The orderlies began prying the wallflowers off the walls, using their nightsticks when necessary. Other patients appeared to know the routine, allowing themselves to be corralled into a sloppy single-file line.

Charlotte maneuvered herself in front of Danny, the person she felt safest turning her back on. Yet she still found herself periodically checking over her shoulder.

When she reached the front of the line, Nurse Ratcliff looked Charlotte up and down. "The new girl." She checked her clipboard and then turned to a young nurse manning the tray of meds. The young nurse gave her a paper cup containing pills. Nurse Ratcliff checked the cup to verify its contents before handing it to Charlotte.

A nurse with jet-black hair took a paper cup of water from her tray and held it out.

Nurse Ratcliff glared at Charlotte until she popped the pills in her mouth and washed them down. When she turned to leave, Nurse Ratcliff grabbed her by the shoulder and spun her around.

"Show me," Nurse Ratcliff said sternly.

Show me? What was she supposed to show her?

She frowned at Charlotte's bewildered expression. Finally, the nurse sighed and gave Charlotte a demonstration. She opened her mouth, then stuck her tongue out and lifted it up.

Charlotte finally understood. She had to prove that she'd swallowed her medication and not secreted it under her tongue. She opened her mouth and revealed that it was empty. Satisfied, Nurse Ratcliff immediately turned her attention to Danny.

Charlotte waited for Danny to take his meds and prove he swallowed them. Despite his scrawny build and mild manner, something about having him near made her feel... safer.

After the last of the inmates received their meds, one of the orderlies shouted, "Line up!"

The patients began dividing themselves into two lines, male and female, and shuffled after their respective white-clad shepherd. The men were herded to the left by the male orderlies, while the women followed the nurses to the right.

Fear gripped Charlotte's chest as Danny left her to join the other men. She suddenly felt abandoned. Vulnerable. Who would have her back now? She wanted to cry out, 'Don't leave me!' but she feared she'd only be proving to the staff that she really was crazy.

Danny glanced back and gave her a quick wave before disappearing around the corner.

Frozen with fear, Charlotte watched the other inmates file out of the common room. An image flashed in her mind of Nurse Stodgy gleefully saying, *Welcome to Eloise.*

Her heart beat against her ribcage as if trying to pound its way out. It was bad enough being surrounded by crazy people during the day, but at night?

Nurse Stodgy's voice continued haunting her. *Where do you think you are, The Grand Hotel?*

A sharp, penetrating blow between her legs propelled her forward. The pain shot up inside her, making her legs wobbly. She glanced back to find a stocky orderly stroking his nightstick with a grin and a wink.

Great. One more predator to watch out for. As if the crazy people weren't bad enough, now she had to worry about an orderly violating her with a two-foot-long nightstick.

Charlotte rushed ahead and merged into the women's line, the dull ache following her. As she fought back the tears, she dreaded what promised to be the longest night of her life.

* * *

As they shuffled down the hallway, Charlotte wondered how many women she would have to share her room with. She wished she had considered this earlier. If she had, she would've positioned herself in line with the less disturbed inmates to improve her chances of getting a decent night's sleep. Not to mention her chances of survival.

When they turned the corner, Charlotte gasped as she stared into the sizeable, dormitory-style room filled with rows and rows of twin beds. There had to be at least fifty of them! A spike of fear pierced her heart, and she began to shake.

How long must she be imprisoned here? Undoubtedly, the doctors and staff would see there wasn't anything wrong with her. Right? Wouldn't they have to let her go? Eventually? But when?

How long had Danny been here, she wondered. She should've asked him. Then again, maybe it was better not to know. What if it wasn't weeks or months? What if he'd been here for *years*? The startling image of the old, toothless woman smiling at her flashed in her mind. Was she destined to become her?

Bleach fumes from the recently mopped floor accosted her nostrils as she began to hyperventilate. The room started spinning.

Pull yourself together, Charlotte! If they saw her having a panic attack, it would only confirm their suspicions and encourage them to extend her stay.

Charlotte almost laughed at that word. *Stay.* Like she was on vacation, and this was a week's stay at a luxury hotel. Charlotte wasn't a guest. She was an inmate. She wasn't here voluntarily. She'd been committed. And there was no *checking out*. You had to be *released*. And not until *they* said so.

The others wandered off to their beds as Charlotte glanced around, confused. Was it every woman for herself, or were there assigned bunks?

The mother with the invisible baby tucked it into bed and kissed it goodnight before crawling under the covers next to it.

A commotion started to her left when one of the patients began jumping on the bed. The black-haired nurse ordered her to get down. After the jumper repeatedly ignored the nurse's threats, she called for Helga, a hulking nurse with broad shoulders, no neck, and blonde hair braided and pinned tight to her head. The floor shook as Nurse Helga stomped over. Her expression showed that she meant business.

"Down!" Nurse Helga yelled in a German accent. The jumping slowed, but the patient continued to bounce.

"I said, Down!" The stocky nurse grabbed the patient's arm in her massive fist. The jumper tried to pull away, but there was no escaping Helga's grip. The black-haired nurse grabbed the jumper's other arm, and the two nurses wrestled with the patient as she shrieked like a train whistle.

Charlotte covered her ears. You would think they were torturing the poor girl the way she carried on.

Nurse Ratcliff huffed, "Oh, for goodness sake!" She pulled a syringe out of her starched-white uniform pocket and marched over. "Hold her still!"

The two nurses did their best to hold the patient steady as Nurse Ratcliff primed the syringe before jabbing it into the jumper's thigh. The patient's shrill cries hit a crescendo.

Charlotte flinched as if she'd been the one the needle was thrust into. *Please, somebody, make her shut up!* Despite pressing her palms to her ears as tightly as possible, Charlotte still couldn't block out the tortured cries.

The nurses mercifully managed to wrestle the jumper to the bed. Helga used her heft and girth to pin her to the mattress as the black-haired nurse strapped the woman to the bed with the leather restraints.

Charlotte flashed back to when she first awoke in this awful place. The claustrophobic feeling of helpless panic gripped her again as if she were still strapped to the bed. Her heart raced. She could hardly catch her breath. *I gotta get out of here. I gotta get out!*

"What are you doing standing around?"

Charlotte recoiled, hearing the voice of the orderly who tried to deflower her with his nightstick. He must've been drawn by all the commotion. "Do I need to get you in your bed myself?"

Charlotte vaulted forward, horrified at the thought of the orderly violating her with his nightstick again.

She glanced around frantically, but the beds all seemed occupied. The thought of some twisted version of musical chairs returned. Only this one featured a nightstick.

Finally, she spotted an open bed and rushed toward it, praying she could claim it before someone else. She practically dove onto the bed. The bedsprings squeaked, but the dense mattress barely gave an inch. What was it stuffed with, sawdust? Despite the lack of comfort, the bed was like an oasis in a sea of insanity.

The bedding was tucked in military tight. Charlotte pried up the army-style blanket and stiff white cotton sheet and slid underneath. The mattress springs shrieked in protest. Pulling the sheet up to her chin, Charlotte clenched it in her fists as if the thin layers of material could provide some magic protection.

"Mr. Hunter!" Nurse Ratcliff called, louder than necessary.

"Yes, ma'am." He answered in a patronizing way.

"I believe we have everything under control here."

"Well, if you ladies need anything," the orderly said, scanning the room, "you just give old Hunter a call." He gave one of the young nurses a wink.

Her face flushed.

"Goodnight, Mr. Hunter," Ratcliff said, shooting a disapproving glance at the blushing nurse.

The orderly grinned and saluted Charlotte with his nightstick, sending a shudder through her body. He swaggered out of the room, whistling and twirling his nightstick. Before the orderly disappeared around the corner, he glanced back one last time as if promising Charlotte that this wouldn't be the last she'd see of him.

Charlotte released a pent-up breath and closed her eyes. The evening meds were kicking in as waves of pharmaceutical relief washed over her.

Someone pushed a cart with a squeaky wheel down the hall.

Hushed voices carried on a brief conversation.

Shoes scuffed the floor before fading away.

A loud click sent the room into darkness, triggering a terrified scream echoing down the hall. What demons must haunt a man to make him wail like that?

Heavy footfalls scuttled past, the screams continuing to echo through the halls.

"Oh God, make it stop! They're crawling all over me! Get them off of me!"

The cries were abruptly stifled. Charlotte was afraid to know how. She squeezed her eyelids shut and let the meds take her away into dreamland.

* * *

Charlotte awakened to the steady rhythm of rain. A low rumble of thunder shook her bed. Ever since she was a young girl, thunder and lightning had always set her on edge. It reminded her of the first time her parents had made her sleep in her own room by herself. Father had put his foot down and told her she had to be a big girl and sleep in her own bed. Even when she awakened from a terrible nightmare, her father would always march her right back to bed.

Charlotte hated that her bedroom was at the other end of the hall from her parents. What if they couldn't reach her before the monsters in the closet got her?

The only exception was when it was storming out. Charlotte's father had grown up in Kansas in what he referred to as *tornado alley*. A twister had torn the roof off his family home when he was a boy. The experience had terrified his family so badly that his father had sold their farm and moved them to central Michigan.

If thunderstorms were enough to scare her stouthearted, mid-western father, what chance did she have?

Even after she married Jack, whenever there was a thunderstorm, she sought the comfort of a reassuring touch. She knew it was silly, but just knowing that she could reach over and feel him beside her provided comfort.

Of course, Jack would often take advantage of her fear and need for emotional support to turn it into an opportunity for sex. But she didn't fight it. It was better than facing the storms of life all alone.

Lightning flashed. Even though her eyes were closed, the brilliant light permeated her eyelids. She waited for the thunder and counted. One... two... three...

Thunder exploded. It was close.

The rumbling reverberated in her chest. Even the bed rattled. Somewhere in the distance, there was a howl.

Charlotte reached for Jack. Felt the warmth of his hairy arm. It calmed her heart and mind. She smiled and opened her eyes, squeezing his sinewy forearm.

Lightning flashed again.

Charlotte screamed.

The arm wasn't Jack's. A wild-haired hag stared back at her with a toothless grin.

Charlotte abandoned the hag's hairy arm like it was a poisonous snake and pulled the sheets up to her chin.

Thunder roared, triggering another howl echoing down the hall.

Another flash of Lightning lit up the room, revealing a host of asylum inmates surrounding her bed. Charlotte screamed. *How long had they been watching her?*

Her eyes slowly adjusted to the gloom as the misshapen silhouettes crowded in on her. Charlotte's heart pounded. Her throat tightened, choking off another scream.

Shadowy arms grasped for her as the dark figures closed in. Her heart hammered in her chest. Charlotte could feel the heat coming off of them. Suffocating her. Blocking out all light until the darkness consumed her.

* * *

Charlotte startled awake to bright sunlight pouring in through the windows. A flurry of commotion whirled all around her. Starched white nurses shouted, rattled keys, and prodded the women out of their beds. Their efforts were met with reluctant groans and defiant shouts.

Charlotte tried to sit up, but her body ached all over.

"Rise and shine, ladies!"

The reality of her surroundings struck her like a speeding locomotive, filling her with dread. Each morning she awakened, it was the same. Expecting to see her carefully decorated bedroom, she was shocked and dismayed to discover herself mired in this deranged, alternate reality.

"Everybody up! You too, princess."

Charlotte looked up to see Nurse Stodgy looming over her. When she tried to sit up again, a piercing pain in her ribs stopped Charlotte cold. It felt like she'd been stabbed. As the numbness of sleep wore off, an assortment of aches and pains cried out for attention.

"Up!" Nurse Stodgy ordered.

Unable to sit up, Charlotte opted to roll out of bed instead.

The day shift nurses rounded up the women and herded them down the hall to the showers. As if showering in front of Nurse Stodgy wasn't bad enough, now she would have to strip naked in front of all the other female patients and nurses as well.

It took three nurses to corral the female patients into the showers. Remembering how long it took for the water to warm up last time, Charlotte let most of the other women go first.

When it came to her turn, Charlotte stripped off her gown and handed it to one of the nurses. The way the nurse gaped at her naked body made Charlotte uncomfortable. It was like she was staring at the aftermath of a horrific car wreck. Sure, Charlotte may have put on a few pounds lately, but there was no way she deserved that kind of reaction.

Charlotte glanced down at herself and gasped. No wonder she hurt all over. Her body was covered with bruises and bite marks. Visions of the inmates crowding around her last night flashed in her mind. *Oh, God! What had they done to her?*

Charlotte looked around at the others, catching knowing glances and guilty grins. She felt dirty. Violated.

A nurse took a used bar of soap from one of the other patients and handed it to Charlotte. Glancing down at Charlotte's injuries, she said, "I see the others have taken a liking to you."

She staggered under an unoccupied shower-head, oblivious to the temperature. What did it matter? She was already numb.

Despite the pain, Charlotte scrubbed her body as if she could erase the purple bruises and scour away the bite marks. Hoping to wash away this nightmare for good to reveal the real Charlotte underneath.

* * *

Charlotte stared through the bars of the common area window overlooking the asylum's manicured lawn, reminding herself that a world existed outside this mental prison. She would give anything to go back to her old life. Even if it meant giving Jack another chance. After all, was she really sure she hadn't imagined the affair? Did she really have any concrete proof?

But if he wasn't cheating on her, then why did he have her committed? To teach her a lesson? What lesson? Not to be so crazy-jealous? And how long would it take for her to *learn her lesson*? Would he even give her another chance? Was it even worth it?

None of it mattered anyway, as long as she was still imprisoned here. How long could they possibly keep her here? Charlotte gazed around the room and glimpsed the wild-haired hag staring at her. Drool oozed from her toothless grin. Charlotte feared she was staring at her future self.

Dread coiled itself like a python around her chest, threatening to squeeze the life out of her.

Charlotte turned back to the window. It dawned on her why they put bars on the windows. If they hadn't, she'd be tempted to get a running start and put an end to this nightmare once and for all.

"Charlotte Davis..."

Her name barely registered through the Muzak droning overhead.

"Will Charlotte Davis please report to the nurse's station?" the staticky voice announced through the overhead speakers.

Did she hear that right? Was she being paged?

Danny shouted, "Charlotte!"

Then, another patient shouted her name.

And another.

Soon, her name was being chanted by more and more of the inmates. "Charlotte! Charlotte! Charlotte!"

Chills ran through her. Why did they want to see her? Did she dare hope that she was finally being released?

"Charlotte Davis, you have a visitor."

The chorus continued, "Charlotte! Charlotte! Charlotte!"

She staggered toward the nurse's station. Who could it be? Who even knew she was in here? Had word gotten back to Joan, and she'd come to rescue her? The way gossip traveled on her street, it was possible. *Dear God, let it be Joan...*

Nurse Leslie escorted Charlotte down the hall to a visitor's room with large observation windows. As the nurse opened the door to let her in, Charlotte's heart leaped in her chest when she saw Jack standing to greet her.

Did he finally have a change of heart? Or did he just miss having someone to take care of him and cook his meals? Maybe he'd run out of clean clothes. But what difference did it make? He was finally here to take her home, and that was all that mattered.

Charlotte rushed up to Jack and threw her arms around him, unable to hold back her tears. She sobbed into his shoulder, clinging to him as if she were hanging onto the edge of a cliff for dear life.

She finally pulled away and wiped the tears from her cheeks. Jack handed her his handkerchief and motioned for them to sit at the table.

"I'm sorry," Charlotte said. "You don't know what it's been like in here."

She dried her eyes and handed the handkerchief back, thanking him.

Jack slid a stack of papers toward her. "Here, you need to sign this."

Charlotte's demeanor brightened. "Is this a release form?"

"Sort of," he said.

Sort of? What did that mean? She skimmed the document. One word jumped off the page. *Divorce.* It was a release form, all right. Just not for her.

Had this been the plan all along? She wanted to throw the papers back in his face. But what choice did she have? He held all the cards. She didn't want to give up her marriage to the only man she'd ever loved. But if this was the only way to escape this nightmare...

But then what?

Charlotte choked back tears, unable to speak. She pleaded with her eyes.

Jack held out a pen.

She stared at the pen as if it were a rattlesnake, unable to move for fear it may strike.

He took her hand and squeezed. Her heart fluttered. Perhaps the flame hadn't completely gone out? Maybe they could still work this out. She managed a weak, hopeful smile.

Jack pulled her hand toward him and placed the pen in it.

She swallowed hard. "Can't we at least talk about this?"

He sighed impatiently.

"I'll do whatever you want. I'll be a better wife, I swear! I can change!" Charlotte began to sob. "Please, Jack. Just tell me what you want from me—"

A knock on the glass startled her. An attractive young blonde peered through the glass at them. When Jack turned his head, she tapped her watch.

It was her! The woman in the restaurant sitting with Jack. It wasn't her imagination after all!

Jack raised a finger to the woman and then turned back to Charlotte. "There's no reason to make this any harder than it needs to be."

Harder? *Harder*! The pen in her fist threatened to snap. She was the one locked up in this hellhole, surrounded by crazy people.

Her thoughts swirled. Certainly, there must be some way to keep Jack from leaving her.

Charlotte gently placed her hand on Jack's cheek. She glanced at the blonde in the window, then ran her fingers through Jack's hair, pulled his face toward hers, and jammed the pen into his eye socket.

A scream echoed through the hallway, barely muted by the glass separating Jack's mistress from them.

Blood streamed down Jack's tortured face. "You bitch!"

Charlotte slammed the heel of her hand into the pen, driving it deep into Jack's frontal lobe. He pitched backward, his chair tipping over. Jack's head bounced off the linoleum with the hollow thud of a dropped bowling ball. His good eye rolled back into his head, but the one with the pen jammed above it just stared straight ahead.

Charlotte turned toward Jack's hysterical mistress and smiled contentedly.

* * *

Charlotte's actions did not go unpunished. Electroshock therapy. Weeks of isolation, observation, and anger management therapy.

Yet, she didn't regret giving Jack what he deserved. Not for a single minute. Of course, Charlotte didn't tell the doctors that. She played their game. By now, she'd figured out the rules. Remain calm. Tell them what they want to hear. Feign remorse.

The day Charlotte was allowed back into the common area, she was careful to control her emotions. Not too high. Not too low. She knew they'd be watching her from the windows of their observation room.

Charlotte scanned the room for familiar faces. The breadcrumb lady was still trying to find her way home. The dancer waltzed around the room without a care in the world. The hand washer was still scrubbing. And the mother with the invisible child was still rocking.

"Charlotte!"

She glanced around, trying to locate the familiar voice.

"Charlotte, over here!"

Someone over at the checkers table waved enthusiastically. It was Danny. He apologized to his opponent and rushed over to embrace her. This time, she let him.

"I—I thought for sure they took you away, and you were gone for good!" He beamed.

"Guess you're stuck with me for a while."

Danny laughed and fidgeted nervously, blushing a little.

Charlotte threw him a lifeline, breaking the awkward moment of silence. "So, what's new?"

"New? Ha! Nothing's ever new around here," he laughed.

Charlotte noticed the man in the wheelchair across the room. Only, he looked... different. Familiar. She shuffled toward him. No. It couldn't be! Her head spun with a whirl of emotions.

As she approached him, Jack gazed up at her with a vacant expression. Then, his head tilted slightly as if in a flash of recognition. Drool trickled down his chin, his mouth moving wordlessly.

Danny said, "Oh, right. He's new. But don't worry about him," Danny said, gesturing with his index figure, mimicking a lobotomy tool puncturing his eye. "He can't hurt you."

Charlotte grinned. "No. Not anymore."

Eye for an Eye

"You sure you know where you're going?" Latisha asked from the passenger seat of Jennifer's Prius. "This don't look like a freeway."

Jennifer shifted in her seat. "What do you expect? We're in fly-over country."

"I expect more than two lanes, that's what."

"Would you prefer L.A. traffic?"

"Shit, at least I'd know we weren't in the middle of a damn zombie apocalypse," Latisha said. "When's the last time you seen another car?"

With no vehicles on the horizon, Jennifer checked the rearview mirror.

Nothing but empty road.

"Look at the bright side," Jennifer said. "Maybe we'll be rescued by Rick Grimes."

"I don't need no man to rescue me." After a moment of silence Latisha added, "Although, if Daryl Dixon showed up..."

They both bust out laughing.

Growing up in Los Angeles, Jennifer had never experienced the open road. Even at two in the morning, L.A. still had traffic. How many times had she been on the 101 freeway and wished she could make all the traffic disappear? And here she was, without another car in sight, and it felt...strange. Unsettling, even.

Jennifer dreaded the drive cross-country, but it was better than spending another semester at college having to bum rides, or worse yet, take public transportation. She'd tried some of those ride-share apps, but most drivers were college guys looking to hook up with coeds. The rest were middle-aged men looking to hook up with coeds.

She had never been outside Southern California before her parents convinced her to enroll in the same Ivy League college where they'd met. As a political science major, it seemed like a good idea to see more of America. It might come in handy for a future essay. Or, if she decided to get involved in national politics, it couldn't hurt to know what life outside L.A. County was like. But deep down, she was a bit nervous driving through so many red states.

"Thanks again for being my co-pilot," Jennifer said. "I think this trip would've driven me crazy doing it alone."

Latisha smiled. "You know I got your back, girl."

Jennifer and Latisha met their freshman year in a gender studies class and hit it off immediately. It wasn't just the SoCal connection. They both shared the same naïve/hopeful/impossible conviction that they were going to save the planet and change the world. *Social Justice Warriors*, her dad called them.

Now, on their third day driving across the United States, the world seemed a whole lot bigger. And Jennifer felt a whole lot smaller.

* * *

Jennifer examined her blue hair in the mirror, thinking it might be time to change the color again. She loved the way it matched the color of her Prius, but maybe it was time to make a bolder statement, like bright red or hot pink? Or maybe green to demonstrate her passion for combating climate change?

The radio station gradually faded into static. Jennifer tweaked the tuning knob but couldn't locate a signal. She tried the scan button to search for a station with a stronger signal, but the numbers just whizzed by without any hits.

Up ahead, a rabbit left the desert scrub and hopped onto the gravel shoulder.

"Finally!" Latisha said. "Some sign of life."

Jennifer looked up from the radio as the rabbit darted into the road.

"Look out!" Latisha shouted.

Jennifer swerved but felt the body crush under her tires. She screamed as if she had been hit by the car.

"Oh-my-god, oh-my-god, oh-my-god!" she shouted, checking the rearview mirror, hoping she hadn't just taken the life of another living thing.

Before reality and the associated guilt had time to set in, an eighteen-wheeler sounded its ear-piercing horn.

The girls screamed in harmony.

The semi's chrome grill raced toward them like a gleaming skyscraper.

Jennifer slammed on her brakes and swerved to the right, over-correcting and skidding onto the shoulder. She tried to pull out of the slide, but the loose gravel caused her to drift sideways. Jennifer cranked the wheel but to no avail.

The Prius barreled through the brush, lurching like a bucking bronco, the scrub clawing at the undercarriage with a metallic shriek.

Their vehicle came to a halt before their screaming did.

Jennifer's heart pounded as she struggled to catch her breath. She released her death grip on the wheel and turned to Latisha.

"Are you okay?"

Latisha stared back, wide-eyed, her lips moving but unable to form words. When the words finally came, they started with an F.

Jennifer took her foot off the brake, but the vehicle didn't budge.

"No, no, no..." There was no way she was going to get stranded out here in the middle of nowhere. Jennifer stomped the accelerator, and the Prius rocked forward. But the tires failed to catch traction.

"Shit!"

Jennifer shifted into reverse and gunned it. The Toyota lurched backward, scraping over the desert scrub before coming to a dead stop.

"You gotta be shittin' me!" Latisha said.

Jennifer alternated between forward and reverse, her panic escalating until the Prius finally jerked free of the brush.

"Yes!"

Free at last, Jennifer pulled back onto the shoulder and stopped.

Latisha frowned. "What're you waitin' for?"

"That poor rabbit!" Jennifer's eyes glistened. "Do you think it's..."

Latisha shook her head.

Still shaken, Jennifer looked both ways. Seeing that the road was clear, she made a quick U-turn.

"What're you doing?" Latisha asked.

"What if she's only wounded? What if she's suffering?"

"Whatcha gonna do, put it out of its misery?"

"No! I mean, I couldn't," Jennifer grimaced. "But maybe if we just, like, nursed it back to health or something."

"I'm a Liberal Arts major," Latisha deadpanned. "Not a rabbitologist."

Jennifer inched back along the highway, her head out the window, watching the asphalt roll by, hoping against hope the rabbit had somehow survived.

Jennifer gasped and slammed on the brakes. The girl's heads jerked forward.

"What the hell was that for?" Latisha complained.

Jennifer gawked at the crimson tire track on the road. She clasped her hand to her breast, her eyes welling with tears. Putting the car in park, Jennifer opened her door and stepped out onto the scorching blacktop, leaving her car in the middle of the highway.

Latisha leaned forward to see what Jennifer was gaping at.

There, in the middle of the road, lay the rabbit, a tire tread flattening its midsection, one eye bulging from its socket, its guts forced out its mouth.

Her stomach lurched as if her insides were going to come out of her mouth, too. She swallowed her bile and let the tears flow.

Jennifer couldn't recall having seen anything dead before. If any animals had gotten run over in her suburban neighborhood, the street sweeper must've whisked it away before she discovered it. Her gaze fixated on the dull, lifeless eye glaring up at her, accusing. Flies buzzed around the carcass, deciding where to lay their eggs.

Why had she been so focused on that damn radio?

She bent over the mangled animal, clutching a set of invisible pearls, oblivious to the SUV barreling toward her.

The SUV's driver leaned on the horn. Jennifer whipped her head around in time to see her life flash before her eyes, the image of herself lying in the road, a filthy tire tread separating her body in half, her guts strewn across the highway.

At the last second, she jumped back, pinning herself to the side of the Prius, evading the three-ton vehicle by mere inches. The wake from the speeding SUV blew back her hair, dirt and asphalt debris pelting her face.

"Jennifer!" Latisha shouted from inside the car. "Are you crazy, girl?"

Jennifer's heart raced like the jackrabbit's must have right before she crushed it beneath her tires. Was this Mother Nature trying to even the score? Karma?

"Get outta the damn road!" Latisha yelled.

"But... I can't just leave her here."

"The hell you can't!" Latisha said. "Girl, there ain't nothin' you can do for that thing."

Jennifer glanced both ways, then took a closer look at the poor creature. "It's not moving."

"Of course it ain't. It's dead! And you'll be too if you don't get your ass outta the road."

Jennifer turned back to Latisha. "Don't you think we should at least give it a proper burial?"

A large black crow suddenly swooped down and landed on the carcass. It pecked at the rabbit's eye socket until it managed to pluck out the eyeball.

Jennifer gawked helplessly, gorge rising in her throat. Her stomach clenched, and she doubled over, retching onto the asphalt. The sour taste of stomach acid made her gag and vomit again.

Latisha came around the vehicle and put her hand on her friend's shoulder.

"You can't fix every injustice in this world, Jen. Some shit just outta your control."

Jennifer trembled.

Latisha stomped her foot and shooed the crow away. "It's survival of the fittest out here, baby girl."

Jennifer's stomach hitched a couple more times. Latisha grabbed Jennifer's hair and held it back for her like she did at that frat party they crashed first semester. Jennifer's whole body shook as she retched one last time.

"C'mon, girl, let's get the hell outta here," Latisha said. "Before *we* become roadkill."

* * *

The faded black ribbon of weather-beaten highway stretched ahead for miles. The drone of the tires and the monotonous terrain lulled Jennifer into a hypnotic, auto-pilot state. Latisha had nodded off long ago, and without her conversation, Jennifer was on the brink of dozing, too.

The radio faded into static again. Jennifer turned it off and slouched further down in her seat, her eyelids growing heavy.

A horn blast startled Jennifer from her slumber as her Prius strayed over the centerline. Her heart leaped in her chest, seeing the RAM pickup truck heading straight at her. Jennifer cut the wheel to the right as the pickup swerved onto the shoulder to avoid a head-on collision.

She was awake now!

Jennifer exhaled the breath she'd been holding hostage and then took a couple deep, cleansing breaths to slow her racing heart. She glanced over at Latisha to apologize, but her eyes were closed, mouth slack. Fortunately, her friend hadn't noticed their latest near-death experience.

Shifting in her seat, Jennifer checked the GPS console for a rest stop or town nearby, hoping to get out and stretch her legs and maybe grab an iced coffee.

The screen was blank.

How was that possible? Could they literally be in the middle of nowhere?

Jennifer grabbed her water bottle and drank liberally until a thought struck her — what if they broke down and this was all the water they had to survive on? Then she remembered the AAA card her father had given her. He'd assured her that all she had to do was call for roadside assistance, and somebody would be there within an hour. She glanced at her smartphone for reassurance.

No reception bars.

Maybe she was just being paranoid. Even without cell service out here, another car or truck would happen by eventually. Right?

A program she'd watched with her mother on the Investigation Discovery channel flashed in her mind. The story was about a college student who had broken down alongside a deserted road, and some creep had pulled over to "help" her. Hikers found the coed's body months later. They never found her head.

Jennifer shuddered. Forcing herself to focus on the road, she decided to pull over at the next rest stop or exit that showed any sign of life. If she could walk around, maybe do some yoga stretches to get the blood flowing, or even splash some cold water on her face, it might wake her up. *Water.* Jennifer made a mental note to grab some more water bottles when she stopped.

The *Add Fuel* alert chimed, startling her from her daze. Jennifer glanced at the console and noticed the last bar on the fuel gauge blinking. How long had it been flashing? It wouldn't be the first time she'd run out of gas. Since the hybrid got such great mileage, she often forgot it didn't just run on wind power. But this time, her father was a thousand miles away.

As the next exit approached, Jennifer looked for signs of food or fuel. But the closer she got, the more it seemed like a crossroad to nowhere. She'd have to wait for the next one.

More exits passed without any hint of civilization. Why did these roads even exist? She supposed they had to lead somewhere, but it sure didn't help her growing feeling of isolation or lessen the possibility of getting stranded on some deserted stretch of road.

Jennifer glanced at Latisha. Still sleeping. Should she wake her? Knowing Latisha, she'd just give her *the look* and then go back to sleep.

The flashing fuel indicator in Jennifer's peripheral vision kept haunting her. It reminded her of those heart monitors you see in hospitals tracking a patient's heartbeat. The kind that eventually flatlined.

Another exit approached. Jennifer squinted her eyes and craned her neck, looking for any clue a gas station might exist on either side of the road. The only structures visible were the dilapidated husks of buildings the sun and weather had beaten into submission, their roofs hunched over and caving in, their occupants long dead and gone. Were these the casualties of climate change her professors warned about?

The fuel indicator continued flashing an S.O.S.

Where were all the buildings? Hell, where were all the people? And what happened to the dangerous overpopulation of the planet she kept hearing about? It sure hadn't reached this godforsaken area.

A faded sign off the road caught her eye. It was hand-painted and hard to read from years of weather-fading and neglect, but she was sure it read "Food & Fuel."

Jennifer eased off the accelerator as the exit approached and surveyed the landscape. Still no gas station visible in either direction. Had it closed like the other abandoned businesses she'd passed? Or was it farther off the highway, obscured by trees?

There! Another faded sign.

Exit Here for Gas & Grub!

Sighing with relief, Jennifer flipped on her turn signal and exited the highway.

* * *

At the end of the exit ramp, Jennifer came to a stop sign. The two-lane road was weathered and cracked like charred alligator skin. It didn't appear to have been paved in decades. Did anyone even drive on it anymore? Apparently, all that money the government was spending on infrastructure hadn't reached this far yet.

She looked both ways but couldn't see any gas stations from the offramp. *Now what*?

"Where are we?" Latisha asked, groggy.

Jennifer nearly jumped out of her skin. "You scared the shit out of me!" It took her a moment to catch her breath. "I'm looking for a gas station."

"You sure you got the right exit?" Latisha asked.

"That's what the sign said." Jennifer craned her neck and finally noticed a weathered sign partially obscured by overgrown brush. What was visible displayed an arrow pointing to the right. "It must be this way... I think."

Jennifer turned south onto the bumpy road.

"While you're looking for a gas station, I'll keep an eye out for guys in white hoods," Latisha said, not entirely joking.

They passed a dirt driveway on the right that disappeared behind the trees. Unlike L.A., where they practically built the houses on top of each other, the next driveway seemed "blocks" away. It was like people here didn't like neighbors.

On her left was nothing but farmland for miles. *But if there's a farm, there must be a farmer, right? And farmers had to get their gas somewhere.*

Suddenly, the Prius lost power. Jennifer mashed her foot down on the accelerator, but the speed continued to decrease to 30... 25... 20... then, even with her foot all the way to the floor, the speedometer maxed out at 18 mph.

"I get you trying to save gas and all, but you drivin' slower than my gramma!" Latisha said.

"I can't help it. It won't go any faster!"

"Say what?"

"It's okay. I've seen it do this before."

Latisha's voice rose several octaves. "We drivin' cross country and you knew this thing got problems?"

"It's not like that," Jennifer argued. "I've only seen it do this like a couple times."

Latisha huffed.

"But only when it's about to run out of gas."

"Oh, that makes me feel *much* better."

As the Prius limped along, Jennifer checked the rearview mirror and startled. The bug-encrusted grille of a beat-up pickup grew in the rear window. It triggered the memory of a road rage incident in L.A. when Jennifer inadvertent-ly cut off a guy driving a jacked-up 4x4. She thought she might die then. It seemed even more likely now.

"What's the matter?" Latisha asked.

"We've got company."

Latisha glanced back. "Shit. Okay, just keep it chill."

"I hope he doesn't think I'm driving this slow on purpose."

"Then roll down your window and wave him around!"

Jennifer pushed the button. The window seemed to take forever to open. The whir of the window motor gave way to rushing wind and the pickup engine's roar. She stuck her arm out and waved them past.

The truck remained on their tail.

"They're not passing," Jennifer said, panic creeping into her voice.

"Probably busy putting on their hoods."

Suddenly, the engine revved, and the pickup roared past. Gravel kicked up by the truck's tires pinged off the Prius' exterior, a cloud of dust filling the car. Jennifer coughed as she fought to roll the window back up.

Latisha shouted, "Assholes!"

As the pickup pulled away into the distance, Jennifer let out a giant sigh. But the relief was short-lived as the low fuel alarm dinged again, reminding them they still needed gas. At least that truck was heading in the same direction. *That had to be a good sign, right?*

Latisha held her phone up to the roof of the Prius, then to the window. When that didn't work, she started smacking it against the dash.

"What are you doing?" Jennifer asked.

"I can't get no damn bars!" A sob escaped Latisha before she stifled it. She was never one to show any sign of weakness. A tear tumbled down her cheek, and she whisked it away.

"Don't worry, there's gotta be a town up ahead. And if we do run out of gas, I'm sure we can borrow some from one of the farmers around here."

"Sounds like a scene from one of them damn Texas Chainsaw Massacre movies."

Jennifer spotted something up ahead. Like a palm tree in a desert oasis, there it was... a sign that read "GAS." But like a mirage, her joy quickly vanished when she spotted the familiar pickup parked at the pumps. But what choice did she have? They had to stop.

Jennifer pulled into the gravel lot and stopped beside an old-fashioned, rust-dappled pump. The gas station looked like something from one of those old black-and-white films or TV shows from last millennium.

Before she could turn off the engine, it stopped on its own.

No turning back now.

Jennifer considered waiting until the guys in the pickup left before refilling. But the sooner she gassed up, the sooner they'd be out of there.

Reluctantly, she unbuckled and exited the car. Jennifer tried to avoid eye contact with the pickup driver, sensing him staring at her. She stole a glance to confirm, then immediately regretted it.

"Nice hair!" he drawled. "You spray paint that yourself?" He snorted out a laugh, displaying a picket-fence smile with most of the slats missing.

She wanted to retort, *Nice teeth, what's the matter, couldn't figure out how to use a bottle opener?* But she didn't want to piss him off. He probably had a shotgun mounted inside his truck.

Jennifer decided it was best to just ignore him. She searched for a place on the gas pump to put her credit card but failed to find a card reader slot. Was it possible this rusty pump was so old that it was made before credit card readers? Even the numbers were manual cylinders like an old slot machine instead of digital.

The pickup's passenger got in on the conversation. "Need help winding that thing back up?"

The two hicks bust out laughing.

How was she supposed to pay? She didn't want to go into the rundown gas station. And she refused to ask the pickup driver for help and fall into the helpless female stereotype. Plus, he gave her the creeps. The last thing she wanted to do was give this yokel any encouragement.

"Need some help?"

Jennifer jumped at the deep voice behind her. She turned to find an unshaven old man, at least fifty, she guessed, wiping his hands on his greasy coveralls and smiling at her. There was a large gap where his front teeth should've been. She wondered if everyone in this town was on meth or just didn't believe in toothbrushes.

"I, uh, couldn't seem to figure out where to pay."

"Oh, don't worry about that, darlin'. Just settle up inside when yer done."

Darlin'? Seriously? She flashed a sarcastic smile. "Thanks."

Jennifer examined the filthy pump handle and hesitated. *Ew!* She opened her car door and reached for some napkins. Latisha gave her a wide-eyed, impatient look.

Retrieving the pump handle with the napkin, Jennifer turned only to realize that she'd forgotten to open the fuel-filler door.

"Need me to show you where to insert that thing?" the attendant asked with a sly grin.

Damn it! Holding the pump handle aloft with one hand, Jennifer opened her car door again and bent over to pull the fuel door lever. She suddenly wished she hadn't worn yoga pants. When she stood up, the attendant's eyes were just where she thought they'd be.

Jennifer removed the gas cap, shoved the nozzle into the receptacle with authority, and squeezed the handle. Now that the attendant saw that she wasn't a helpless female, maybe he'd return to his cave.

Glancing back at the pump, Jennifer noticed that the numbers weren't changing. She released the handle and tried again. Nothing. The attendant's gap-toothed smile widened. Jennifer's face grew flush.

The gas station attendant reached over and lifted the lever on the side of the pump. The counters on the pump whirred to life, spinning back to zero. Score one for the patriarchy.

"There you go, darlin', try it again."

Behind her, the pickup driver and his passenger roared with laughter.

Jennifer pursed her lips and gave it another try. Gasoline finally began rushing through the nozzle.

"Just settle up inside after yer done." The gas station attendant moseyed back toward the station, shaking his head. Jennifer pictured him telling the story to his buddies over a beer tonight about the helpless city girl who couldn't even pump her own gas.

She watched the mechanical cylinders count out the gallons. The old pump seemed slower than the modern ones. Or was it just her impatience to get the hell out of there?

The pickup driver finally finished topping off and headed for the station.

Could this pump be any slower?

A hawk circled overhead. Or was it a vulture searching for carrion?

The sun hung low in the sky. At this rate, she might not finish fueling until after dark. They'd want to find a place for the night soon. Someplace as far away from here as possible.

The door to the station opened, and the pickup driver reappeared, smacking a pack of Marlboro Reds against his palm. Jennifer tried to keep her eyes glued to her car but, out of reflex, glanced up as he passed. He shot her a wink and a nicotine-stained checkerboard smile. That image was going to haunt her dreams tonight.

The driver got into his truck and slammed the door, rattling the rusted panels. The engine turned over, and gravel popped under the tires as the pickup pulled out of the lot and sped off. The passenger waved his arm out the window mockingly.

Finally, the nozzle jumped in her hand as the tank reached its limit. She gave the handle one more squeeze to top off the tank before replacing the handle. It was shocking to see how much cheaper the gas was here than in California. Maybe things were beginning to look up after all.

* * *

The grease-smudged gas station door, plastered with Marlboro, Camel, and Lucky Strike stickers, didn't budge at first push. Jennifer had to put her weight behind it and shove. A bell clattered overhead as she wrestled her way inside.

The gas station attendant gave one of those dopey smiles men give to pretty girls. She forced herself to gaze at his grease-stained coveralls so she wouldn't have to see that gap-toothed grin again. A patch on his chest revealed his name was Ralph.

Refrigerator units with smudged glass doors hummed to her right. She'd almost forgotten the water. Her shoes made a sticky sound on the linoleum, making her skin crawl. It didn't look like the floors had been mopped since the fifties. She wondered if she might need a tetanous shot after this.

Opening the refrigerator door, Jennifer looked for coconut water but had to settle for a couple of generic bottles of spring water. She had never wanted out of anyplace more in her life.

She set the plastic bottles on the counter, and Ralph rang her up on an old push-button register that better resembled a vintage typewriter. His whiskers looked like a wire brush pushing through tanned, wrinkled leather.

"It's amazing you stay in business being so far off the main highway," Jennifer said.

"Back in the day, this was the highway," he said. "That'll be $32.75."

She held out her card by the edges, hoping to avoid any physical contact with the man.

"Cash or check only."

Jennifer gawked at the man.

"You don't take credit cards?"

"Nope. Never have."

"W—well, I don't think I have that much cash on me."

A bolt of panic erupted inside her.

"You can use a check. I suppose I can trust you." He said with a wink.

Jennifer had a checking account somewhere that her parents made deposits in every month but she'd never actually written a check from it. Wasn't that what debit cards were for?

"Can I use my debit card?"

"No plastic. Just cash or check." The clerk's smile began to fade.

Jennifer shoved her hands in her pockets but could produce only a folded-up five and two singles.

"Do you have an ATM?" Jennifer asked, looking around.

"A what?"

"An ATM. You know, one of those... automatic... money machines?"

The clerk looked at her like she'd asked if he had a money tree out back. He glanced at the bills in her hand. Then his gaze traced its way slowly up to her face. The smile returned. "If you ain't got enough money," he said, "I reckon we *could* figure out another way for you to... work it off."

Jennifer's heart skipped a beat. The thought of the greasy, toothless old man touching her made her stomach churn. She reached into her pocket for her phone but realized she'd left it in the car. So much for calling 9-1-1. Then again, what would she tell them? That a gas station clerk wouldn't let her leave without paying? And even if she got to her phone, it probably wouldn't work out here, anyway. She had to think of something... and quick.

"I... my wallet is in the car. With my friend." *That was good.* It showed him there was a witness if he tried something. "I'll be right back."

Jennifer grabbed the water bottles, but they didn't budge. The clerk held them in a vice-like grip. His voice deepened, and his eyes locked with hers. "You can pick these up when you come back to pay."

She released the water bottles and stepped back from the counter. "Oh, right."

Turning on her heel, Jennifer power-walked out of the gas station toward the car, careful not to look like she was making a run for it. Deep down, she knew she didn't have that much cash but hoped she was somehow mistaken. Who uses cash anymore?

The distance to the car seemed to have lengthened. She could feel the clerk's eyes on her.

Seeing Latisha in the passenger window eased Jennifer's fears a bit. Maybe *she* had some cash. Or at least, between the two of them, they'd be able to scrounge up enough and then have a good laugh about it later.

Jennifer opened the driver-side door and reached into the back seat for her purse.

Latisha asked, "What are you doing?"

"Quick, see how much cash you got."

"Why don't you just use your credit card?"

Jennifer rifled through her purse. "They don't take plastic." She located her wallet and flipped it open. The billfold was empty. "Shit! Tell me you got some cash on you."

Latisha gave her a look and then dug through the purse at her feet. Retrieving her wallet, she pulled out a ten-dollar bill and held it up.

Jennifer had never been good at math, like her sister, but even she could add ten plus seven. And it added up to trouble. "That's not enough."

"What?"

"We don't have enough cash to pay for our gas!"

Latisha asked, "Then what the hell we supposed to do?"

"I don't know!" Jennifer fought back tears. "The gas station creep said we could 'work it off.'"

"Fuck that," Latisha said.

Just then, the door to the gas station opened, and Ralph emerged, strolling toward them.

"Oh-my-God, here he comes."

Latisha turned to look.

Fear drove a spike into Jennifer's chest. "Whatta we do?"

Latisha said, "Fuck it. Just go."

"What? Are you crazy?"

The clerk closed half the distance between them.

"You want to work it off?" Latisha said.

The gravel crunching under his work boots grew louder.

Jennifer felt paralyzed.

"Just get in the car," Latisha said.

He closed three-quarters of the distance.

"Jen, let's go."

Jennifer sifted through her purse again. "Are you sure you don't have any more cash?"

Latisha glanced back at the man carrying the large wrench. She rummaged through her purse, eventually dumping it into her lap.

Jennifer sat in the driver's seat and yanked open the center console, desperately searching for hidden treasure.

Latisha looked up at the greasy coveralls approaching and frantically pressed the electric door locks.

But they wouldn't lock.

She realized that Jennifer still had her door open. "Close the fucking door!"

Glancing up, Jennifer saw Ralph's grease-stained coveralls fill the passenger window. She grabbed her door and slammed it shut. Just as the clerk bent down to peer into the window, the door locks clicked.

A loud rapping on the passenger-side window made Jennifer jump.

Latisha cried out, "Just go! Go, go, go!"

Panicking, Jennifer fired up the Prius, shifted into drive, and punched the accelerator. The car lurched, spraying gravel and leaving behind a cloud of dust. Rocks pinged off the undercarriage as she spun onto the road heading toward the highway.

Jennifer's heart raced, eyes wide, her foot still pressed to the floor. Latisha whooped and hollered, "Woo! Fuck yeah!"

The Prius's front end dipped, catching a pothole that sent a shudder through the vehicle. Jennifer glanced at the rearview mirror.

No one appeared to be chasing them.

She eased off the accelerator slightly. "What if he calls the cops?"

Latisha scoffed. "Are you kidding? By the time that old white dude figures out how to use a phone, we'll be in the next state."

Jennifer checked the mirror again. Her heart rate began to slow. She'd never stolen anything before, except for a handful of granola or some grapes from the Whole Foods store. And then there was the time she palmed a lipstick when she was thirteen, but she'd been just a kid.

Something appeared in the rearview mirror.

Probably just her imagination.

She checked again.

That something looked bigger.

Closer.

Up ahead, farmland stretched on and on. Had they actually ventured that far off the freeway?

The object in the rearview mirror gained on them. It looked like a truck.

Relax, she told herself. It wasn't the first truck they'd seen on this road. Okay, it was the second.

"I think we got company," Latisha said.

Jennifer watched her rearview mirror as the truck closed on them. Where was the stupid freeway?

The truck's grill quickly eclipsed the rear window. The diesel engine rattled so loud Jennifer could feel it. She didn't know whether to speed up or slow down and encourage the driver to go around.

The highway overpass finally came into view.

The truck's engine roared roared as it surged alongside the Prius. Faded, hand-painted lettering on the side of the truck read "Ralph's Towing Service."

Her heart skipped a beat.

The tow truck catapulted around her, rattling her windows. The exhaust pipe belched a black cloud of smoke, obscuring her vision. When the noxious cloud dissipated, she saw the red tail lights.

Jennifer slammed on the brakes. In all the excitement, they had both forgotten to buckle up. Jennifer's neck snapped forward, and her chest smashed against the steering wheel, sounding the horn. Latisha's head and elbows caromed off the windshield.

The girls gaped at the tow truck stopped dead in the road. The truck door slammed, and the gas station attendant pounded toward them, scowling, a large wrench in his hand.

Unable to form words, Latisha repeatedly smacked her friend's arm. But Jennifer didn't need to be told. She had the Prius in reverse before she even glanced back to see if it was safe.

Watching the backup camera display, she sped away from the tow truck as fast as the Prius would take her.

Another vehicle approached from behind, forcing Jennifer to slam on the brakes again.

"Damn it!"

Up ahead, Ralph hopped back in his tow truck and shoved it in reverse, barreling toward them.

What should she do? If she did nothing, they'd get sandwiched. And after their experience in the desert, she knew the Prius wouldn't make it far off-roading.

The tow truck sped toward them. Latisha shouted, "Jen, do something!"

She froze, unable to decide on the best course of action before the tow truck's tail lights blazed red and its tires screeched.

Jennifer opened her mouth to scream when the tow truck skidded to a halt mere inches from her front bumper.

Before Jennifer could catch her breath, a siren sounded behind her, and the inside of the car illuminated with flashing red light.

She watched her mirrors as Police Chief Walter Ferguson exited his patrol car and strolled to the driver's side window. He rapped his knuckles on the glass so loudly that Jennifer feared he might shatter the window. Already shaking, Jennifer shifted into park and lowered the window.

"License and registration, please."

As Jennifer sifted through her purse, Latisha struggled to find the record button on her iPhone.

"Do you know why I pulled you over, ma'am?"

Latisha piped up, "Was it because we look like we from outta town? Or you just see a black face go by while you hiding in the bushes?"

The officer leaned down to see who was doing all the talking. His reflective sunglasses concealed his eyes. His stoic expression revealed nothing.

"That's right," Latisha said, "I'm recording this whole damn thing."

Jennifer shot Latisha a look. "I'm sure the officer is just doing his job."

She grabbed her purse from the back seat and dug out her driver's license and registration.

"Here you go, officer," Jennifer said as she handed her documentation through the window.

The police chief rose and began writing in his notepad. "I pulled you ladies over because your vehicle matched the description of a car seen fleeing the scene of a crime."

"That's bullshit," said Latisha. "You ain't got no proof."

Just then, Ralph stepped in front of the Prius. "That's them, Walt!"

Jennifer's throat tightened. They were busted. Her only hope was to try to talk her way out of it. She switched to her sweet, innocent voice, the one that had gotten her high school science teacher to give her an A- instead of a B+.

"Excuse me, Mr. Officer. I believe there's been a ginormous misunderstanding here."

Chief Ferguson continued to scribble in his notepad.

"You see, we were about to like, run out of gas, okay. So we stopped to fill up. But when we tried to pay, that man said he wouldn't take our cards. And I'm like, are you serious? So we looked through our wallets and everything, but like, who carries cash anymore? So we went to find an ATM. Then, this guy practically runs us off the road! And that's when you came to our rescue."

Jennifer wet her lips with her tongue and gazed up at the police chief with her doe-like eyes. She hadn't met a man that could say no to that look. It'd already gotten her out of at least two speeding tickets in L.A.

"Please step out of the vehicle, ma'am."

The chief's emotionless delivery made the hairs on the back of her neck stand up. She turned to Latisha. "Okay, let's just do what the officer says, all right. Maybe he'll let us off with just like a warning."

"Fuck that shit, I know my rights. It's not our fault that redneck won't take credit," Latisha huffed. "Probably still use Confederate money 'round here."

"Ma'am, please exit the vehicle."

Jennifer stepped out of the car. Her first thought was how huge the officer was. He must have at least a foot on her. His square jaw looked carved out of stone, and his skin made from leather. She switched from her sexy look to her pouty face — the one that always got her out of being grounded.

In her most innocent girl's voice, she said, "Honest, officer. This is just like a massive misunderstanding. If you can show us where the closest ATM is, I can get the cash, and then you'll never have to see us again, I swear. Besides, I'm sure you got way more important things to worry about than a couple college girls."

"Turn around and place your hands on the vehicle."

Jennifer gawked at the officer a moment before complying.

Chief Ferguson frisked her with his meaty, calloused hands. It felt as if they could crush her like an insect. He grabbed one of Jennifer's wrists and twisted it behind her back before cuffing it to the other.

"Ow, what are you doing?" Jennifer demanded.

"You're under arrest for petty theft. You are also being cited for driving fifty in a thirty-five and for operating a motor vehicle without a seat belt."

Ralph smiled and began hooking the Prius up to his tow truck.

Latisha exploded out of the passenger door and charged at Ralph. "Oh, hell no. There ain't no way you towing our car. Unhook this shit now, or I'm gonna fuck you up."

Ralph regarded Latisha, unable to hide his amusement.

Latisha turned back to the officer. "He ain't got no right to do this. You better make him stop this shit, or so help me—"

The officer led Jennifer toward the back of his cruiser. She stared at Latisha with a wide-eyed look of helplessness.

As Chief Ferguson locked Jennifer in the back of his cruiser, Latisha came tearing around the squad car holding out her iPhone. "What the hell you think you're doing?"

He raised one hand out in front of him while his other hand reached for his service revolver. "Ma'am, you need to step back and keep your hands where I can see them."

Latisha stopped but held her ground. "What're you gonna do, shoot me?"

"I suppose that's up to you."

For once, she was speechless.

"Place your hands on the hood," the Chief said, his hand still on the pistol grip.

Latisha complied, setting her iPhone on the hood, still recording.

Chief Ferguson maneuvered behind her and kicked her legs apart.

"Hey!" she protested.

The officer patted her down, turned the pockets of her denim shorts inside out, and then proceeded to cuff her.

"What the hell is this shit?" Latisha said.

Ralph finished hooking up the Toyota and pulled a lever, lifting the front end off the ground with a whine of hydraulics.

Chief Ferguson steered Latisha toward the back of the cruiser, leaving her iPhone on the hood.

"Wait, I need my phone!" Latisha said.

The officer ignored her plea. He opened the cruiser's back door and pushed her head down. Depositing her in the backseat, he slammed the door shut, rocking the cruiser.

Ralph shouted, "See ya at the station, Walt!"

Chief Ferguson gave him a nod before climbing behind the wheel of the squad car and making a U-turn.

* * *

The police car cruised down the local Main Street. To Jennifer, it looked like they'd entered a town from one of those old black-and-white Twilight Zone episodes. Some of the storefronts looked like they'd been boarded up for a while. She didn't recognize the names of any of the shops that were left.

A lovely woman in a knee-length dress and hair done up strolled along the sidewalk. When she saw the police cruiser, she waved and smiled. As they passed her, Jennifer gasped. The woman's front teeth were missing like everyone else she'd seen in this town.

Up ahead, a brawny man with a handlebar mustache and dark, slicked-back hair stood outside the barbershop, smoking a cigar. As the smoke cloud dissipated, he grinned and winked, the late afternoon sun glinting off his gold tooth.

Jennifer and Latisha glanced at each other nervously.

As the police cruiser approached a two-story brick building with weathered concrete steps, Jennifer's heart sank. Were those bars on the windows? The cruiser turned past the building and parked in the rear.

Chief Ferguson stepped out from behind the wheel and opened the back door of the cruiser to let Jennifer out. After a moment, the Chief leaned down to peer into the back seat.

Latisha said, "I ain't goin' nowhere until I get my phone."

"I can escort you into the station or drag you. It's your choice."

Latisha just sat there, scowling.

"Latisha, you're not helping the situation," Jennifer hissed.

"This is bullshit!" Latisha said but eventually huffed and emerged from the cruiser at her own reluctant pace.

Chief Ferguson led his two prisoners through the back door of the station. The female dispatcher behind the counter was likely in her 40s but had one of those pack-a-day faces that made her look decades older. As they approached the counter, she gave a half-smile.

"What do we have here?" Alice Ferguson said in a raspy smoker's voice, speaking in an oddly affected way.

Chief Ferguson responded, "Filled up at Ralph's and tried to skip out without paying."

"That's bullshit," Latisha said, "I want a lawyer."

A young deputy hanging out in the back snapped his head around at Latisha's words as if she'd shouted "fire." Alice gaped at her as if in shock, revealing her nicotine-stained teeth, except for the two missing on the bottom. She quickly closed her mouth.

"I—I'll write 'em up," Alice said in that same affected way.

Jennifer finally realized what was wrong with her speech. The woman was trying to speak without revealing her missing teeth.

Chief Ferguson signed the girls in on a clipboard and steered them over to a bench. "Have a seat, ladies."

Glancing toward the young officer, Chief Ferguson said, "Jacobs. Check these young ladies in while I write up my report."

The baby-faced officer hitched up his gun belt and stood a little straighter. His chest swelled, and his arms flared out as he accepted his assignment. "Yes, sir, Chief."

Officer Jacobs strutted over to the girls and looked them over. His brown hair was trimmed neatly around his ears and off his collar, clean-shaven except for an underdeveloped mustache.

He motioned to Jennifer. "Ma'am, do you mind steppin' over here?"

Jennifer stood wide-eyed.

Latisha said, "Can't you just tell us what we owe so we can pay and get the hell out of this shit-hole town?"

Officer Jacobs flinched. He blinked a few times as if trying to compute what she'd said. After glancing over his shoulder, he leaned in close and whispered, "Y'all might want to exercise your right to remain silent. You don't know what you're—"

"You ain't silencing me. I know my rights."

"Ma'am, you don't understand how much trouble y'all are in here," Jacobs said under his breath. "You could see *the chair.*"

"What?" Jennifer said, incredulous. "You mean, like, the electric—"

"Is there a problem, Jacobs?" the Chief called across the room.

"Um, no, sir," Jacobs replied, then turned back to Jennifer. "Please follow me, ma'am."

Officer Jacobs uncuffed Jennifer's hands and led her over to a table where he began fingerprinting her, his back to the rest of the office.

Keeping his voice down, he said, "Listen. I'm trying to do y'all a favor." Jacobs peeked over his shoulder.

Jennifer lowered her voice. "Why can't we, like, pay a fine or something and just go?"

"It doesn't work like that here," Jacobs said. "There are laws on the books that—" Reading Jennifer's face, Jacobs stopped. The front desk dispatcher strolled by and busied herself at the nearby file cabinets, eavesdropping.

Jacobs finished fingerprinting Jennifer and led her back to Latisha, who scowled up at him. "Okay, ma'am," Jacobs said. "If you can come with me."

Latisha eyeballed him for an uncomfortable moment, then finally stood. "All right, let's get this shit over with."

Officer Jacobs fingerprinted Latisha and returned for Jennifer before escorting them to an empty holding cell and unlocking it.

"Are you for reals?" Latisha asked.

Jacobs motioned them into the cell and they reluctantly complied. The metal door clanged shut behind them with an uncomfortable sound of finality.

* * *

"Hello?" Jennifer called out through the bars, her voice echoing off the concrete walls of the jail cell. "Excuse me."

Latisha stood up from the bench she'd been lying on. "Yo! Ain't we supposed to get a phone call or something?" she shouted. "Hey! I want a lawyer!"

"Well, whaddya know? Looks like I'm just in time." An older, overweight man approached, wearing a crooked tie and a light gray suit that he appeared to have slept in. His used car salesman's smile seemed to include all his teeth, although it was questionable if they were originals.

Jennifer and Latisha traded sideways glances.

"Let me introduce myself. The name's Aiden Fletcher, Attorney at Law." He handed a business card through the bars.

Latisha said, "Well, Mr. Fletcher, Attorney at Law, you aware that we been deprived our right to make a phone call?"

Fletcher grinned. "Unless you or your daddies already have a local lawyer on retainer, I wouldn't waste my time making that phone call. It would merely prove to extend your stay here in these..." Fletcher gazed around the cell. "Meager accommodations."

Jennifer said, "If we're gonna be stuck here, like overnight, I'll need to call my parents and let 'em know. If they don't hear from me, they're gonna be worried."

"Indeed, indeed." Fletcher nodded. "Fortunately for you, we believe in swift justice in these parts."

Jennifer shot a wary glance at Latisha.

"As long as you do what I tell you," Fletcher said, "We should have you on your way in no time at all."

Jennifer let out a big sigh. "Oh, Mr. Fletcher, that would be awesome. It really is just a crazy misunderstanding."

Fletcher smiled as if he'd heard that before.

"So what do we do now?" Jennifer asked.

"Leave everything to me," Fletcher said. "I've already secured a court date for this evening. You young ladies just sit tight, and I'll see you over at the courthouse."

* * *

Jennifer and Latisha were awakened by a metallic clatter and a screeching hinge. The streetlight outside the lone window cast ominous shadow-bars across the cell. Jennifer sat up.

"Okay, ladies, it's showtime!" Deputy Jacobs said, removing the large metal key from the unlocked cell door.

Latisha rose and stretched her back. "You couldn't have put us in a cell with a bed in it?"

"Those are reserved for our overnight guests," Jacobs said.

Outside, a bell began to toll.

"C'mon ladies, y'all don't want to make the justice of the peace wait, believe me."

* * *

The young officer led Jennifer and Latisha out the rear door of the police station in cuffs as the bell continued to toll. After placing the girls in the back of his cruiser, Jacobs pulled onto Main Street.

The squad car kept to the 25 mph speed limit as Jennifer stared out the windows, disturbed by the sight of townsfolk emerging from buildings and side streets, drawn by the clanging bell. Were they being summoned to the local church for a mid-week service or perhaps a town meeting? The gathering crowd reminded her of a horde of zombies.

The police car slowed as it neared the courthouse, which looked like it had been built a hundred years ago, with its faded red brick and peeling white gables disfigured by years of inclement weather. Jennifer couldn't wait to get this over with and leave this bizarre town in her review mirror.

Officer Jacobs turned into the lot next to the courthouse and stopped abruptly. Jennifer's neck snapped forward. Latisha yelled, "Hey!"

Jacobs honked his horn at a lanky old man in overalls but no shirt, moseying in front of the squad car. The man laughed like it was the funniest thing he'd ever seen. As the cruiser inched past him, the geezer bent down to look into Jennifer's window with wild eyes and a gaping, toothless grin.

* * *

"All rise for the honorable Justice Grimshaw!" The bailiff called.

The murmur from the packed courtroom came to an abrupt halt.

Fletcher rose and glanced down at his clients, who were still seated. He motioned for them to stand. Jennifer stood first, glancing around nervously. Latisha rolled her eyes and then reluctantly rose.

The sober-looking judge shuffled into the courtroom clothed in a long, black robe. He appeared to be well into his sixties. His sparse comb-over presided over thick eyebrows fixed in a permanent scowl.

Fletcher whispered to his clients, "Remember what I said. Let me do the talking. Just sit there and... try to look innocent."

Jennifer flinched when the gavel slammed and echoed through the courtroom. When the bailiff instructed them to sit. Jennifer stole a glance behind her at the packed gallery. The old man in the overalls gave her another gummy grin and a wink. Is life that dull in this hick town that the entire population has nothing better to do than hang out at the courthouse?

The justice asked for the bailiff to read off the charges against Latisha.

"The defendant is charged with 14 counts of moral turpitude," the bailiff announced.

Fletcher stood faster than Jennifer thought possible. "Your honor, as I'm sure you're well aware, the maximum number of moral turpitude charges has been capped at seven based on the decision of Jackson vs City Council."

"Duly noted. The court amends the charges to seven counts of moral turpitude," the Justice said. "How does your client plead, Mr. Fletcher?"

"Your honor, based on the non-violent nature of the offenses and seeing that this child is barely nineteen and likely not familiar with local statutes, my client would like to throw herself on the mercy of the court and ask for his grace and leniency."

"Let the record show that Miss..." the judge leaned over to check his notes before slowly enunciating her name, "La-tish-a Ma-ya Cole pleads guilty to seven counts of moral turpitude—"

Latisha leaped to her feet. "Fuck that shit! I ain't admitting to nothing!"

The crowd behind her gasped. One elderly lady fainted, causing an even greater stir. The justice pounded his gavel, calling for order in the court.

Latisha turned to her court-appointed attorney. "What the hell you getting' paid for? Ain't you gonna at least try to prove me innocent?"

Jennifer shook her head, speechless.

Fletcher reprimanded Latisha under his breath. "Miss Cole, sit down. We agreed you'd let *me* do the talking."

"That was before you rolled over like a little bitch and didn't even try defending me. Ain't you supposed to be a *defense* attorney?"

People in the gallery gasped again, hearing the word "bitch." The toothless old man in the overalls burst out laughing.

The judge pounded his gavel to bring the courtroom under control.

Latisha scowled and plopped into her seat, crossing her arms.

"So which is it, Mr. Fletcher?" the Justice asked. "Is your client pleading guilty or not?"

Fletcher leaned over and whispered to Latisha. "Miss Cole, you are putting me in a rather difficult position."

"Sorry to make you do your job," Latisha said.

"Mr. Fletcher!" The justice barked.

Fletcher stood, stone-faced. "Your honor, my client has decided to plead... not guilty."

* * *

The bespectacled scarecrow of a prosecutor called Ralph Tucker, the gas station attendant and resident tow truck driver, to the stand. The bailiff presented Ralph with a black leather Holy Bible. "Repeat after me, 'Eye for an eye, tooth for a tooth, I swear to tell the absolute truth, so help me God.'"

Ralph swore the oath and took a seat, flashing his gap-toothed grin at the girls.

The prosecutor prompted Ralph to recount the number of times he witnessed Latisha curse in public, and he gleefully complied.

"No further questions, your honor." The prosecutor took his seat.

The girl's public defender patted Latisha on the shoulder and stood, adjusting his suit coat. He approached the witness slowly, gazing upward as if looking to Almighty God for divine intervention or at least guidance. Then Fletcher paused, nodded, and turned his back to the witness. He spoke toward the gallery in a voice low enough for only the first few rows to hear. "How many times did you hear my client use profanity?"

"I beg your pardon?" Ralph said.

Fletcher smiled. He repeated the question slightly louder before turning to the witness for the answer.

"I still didn't quite catch that," Ralph said.

"I see," said Fletcher. "My apologies. Exactly how long have you struggled with your hearing, Mr. Tucker?"

"Objection, your honor!" The prosecutor shouted, leaping to his feet. "The defense is playing games with the witness."

"It's a valid question, your honor," Fletcher said. "The ability of the witness to hear my client is integral to corroborating the charges."

"Just try and speak up so we can *all* hear you, counselor," said the justice.

Fletcher did his best to cast doubt on Ralph's ability to hear Latisha. How far away was he? Wasn't it windy out? How clearly could he possibly hear over the roar of the tow truck's diesel engine and the whine of the hydraulic lift?

Ralph stammered increasingly with each measure of doubt presented. Finally reaching the apex of frustration, Ralph shouted, "I know what I heard!"

Fletcher turned back to the gallery and said in a low voice, "Or what you wanted to hear."

"What did you say?" Ralph shouted.

The prosecutor stood. "Objection!"

Fletcher smiled, "No further questions, your honor."

The prosecutor next called Chief Ferguson to the stand. Chief Ferguson swore the same oath and proceeded to recount fourteen violations he witnessed Latisha commit.

Fletcher approached the witness for cross-examination. "Are you absolutely sure about the number of obscenities you've allegedly witnessed my young client utter? Is it possible that it wasn't fourteen but perhaps twelve? Or ten? Are you willing to swear under threat of perjury that you heard my client utter exactly fourteen obscenities?"

Chief Ferguson paused and replied, "No, sir."

Fletcher turned to the justice. "Your honor, if this witness cannot with any certainty swear to the number of infractions he witnessed, then how can we be certain his testimony is credible? Isn't it possible he misunderstood my client entirely?"

"You didn't let me finish, Mr. Fletcher," Chief Ferguson said. "The prosecutor asked what I heard during the traffic stop. You asked how many obscenities I witnessed, *period*. So counting the outburst by your client right here in this courtroom, then I've witnessed at least *sixteen*."

Fletcher's shoulders dropped. "No further questions for the witness."

The prosecutor gave his closing statements pointing to the credibility of the primary witness, Chief Ferguson, and the fact that they were all witnesses to Latisha's obscene outburst only moments ago, leaving zero doubt as to her guilt.

Fletcher closed with an appeal to Latisha's upbringing in the Sodom and Gomora of California, where spicy words like those allegedly uttered are commonplace. "Is it right," he asked, "that we treat a sojourner in our town this way? I believe the answer can be found in the good book!"

Lifting a worn, brown leather copy of The Holy Bible, Fletcher read from Leviticus 19:33-34. "'And if a stranger sojourn with thee in your land, ye shall not vex him. But the stranger that dwelleth with you shall be unto you as one born among you, and thou shalt love him as thyself; for ye were strangers in the land of Egypt: I am the Lord your God.'"

With that, Fletcher shut the good book with a sound of finality and said, "I rest my case." Fletcher sat with authority, smiling confidently, then crossed his legs as if tying a neat little bow on the case.

The justice of the peace appeared to mull over the evidence presented and the closing statements. Jennifer and Latisha traded glances, wondering what would happen next.

The justice said, "Will the defendant please rise?" Latisha looked at Fletcher, and he nodded. Fletcher stood, and Latisha reluctantly followed.

Justice Grimshaw's eyebrows raised. "Mr. Fletcher, I agree with your assessment."

Fletcher perked up. Jennifer glanced hopefully at Latisha.

The Justice continued. "The stranger should be treated just as 'one born among us.'" Then his thick eyebrows dropped. The room suddenly felt like a black storm cloud descended. "And based on the credibility of the witnesses and the confirmation of the defendant's vulgar outburst here in my court, I find the defendant guilty of the maximum seven counts of moral turpitude." Justice Grimshaw punctuated the ruling with the slam of his gavel.

Jennifer jumped at the sound.

The toothless old man behind her guffawed as if he'd been cheering for a guilty verdict. "Give her the chair!" he shouted.

The gallery called for justice with shouts of "Guilty!" and "Chair!" rising above the clamor.

The judge pounded his gavel and called for order in the court.

The bailiff stepped forward. "The next defendant, Miss Jennifer Ann White, is charged with the crimes of petty theft, fleeing the scene of a crime, speeding, and driving without a seatbelt."

Justice Grimshaw asked, "How does the defendant plead?"

Fletcher stood. "Your honor, my client wishes to plead no contest to the charges of speeding and driving without a seatbelt and is willing to pay any applicable fines."

"Duly noted," said the judge, jotting it down.

"As to the charges of petty theft and fleeing the scene of a crime, the defendant would like to plead... not guilty."

The prosecutor called Ralph Tucker back to the stand. After being reminded that he was still under oath, the prosecutor asked him to describe today's events. Tucker recounted how, after he helped the young lady pump her gas, she and her foul-mouthed friend sped off without paying.

The prosecution rested.

Fletcher rose and moseyed over to cross-examine the witness. He gestured toward Jennifer as he spoke while she gave the most innocent look she could manufacture. "Isn't it true that my client here offered to pay you for the gas, but you refused to take her money?"

Ralph swallowed hard and glanced up at Justice Grimshaw.

"It's a simple yes or no answer, Mr. Tucker," Fletcher said.

"I told her how much she owed, and she pretended to go to her car to get the money, but then she done took off like a bat out of... H-E-double-hockey-sticks." Ralph said.

"You didn't answer my question, Mr. Tucker. Yes or no, did Miss White offer to pay you for the gas?"

"I told that girl I don't take plastic."

Fletcher turned to the justice. "Your honor..."

"Just answer the question, Ralph." The justice said.

"She wanted to use a credit card. I told her I only accept cash or check. And that's when she done run off!"

"So, as you can see, Your Honor, my client offered to pay, but the witness refused to take a perfectly valid method of payment, legal tender in every state of our blessed union." Fletcher threw up his hands. "No more questions for the witness."

"But she took off without paying!" Ralph objected, his face reddening.

"You are dismissed." The justice said to Ralph.

Ralph scowled as he stepped down from the stand, then proceeded to plop down in the front row and crossed his arms.

The prosecutor called Chief Ferguson back to the stand, who described how he responded to a robbery call and caught the defendant speeding away from the scene of the crime.

Fletcher jumped to his feet. "Your honor, my client has already conceded to the charge of speeding, I don't see the need to drag this proceeding out—"

The prosecutor countered, "Your honor, I am trying to establish the fact that the defendant was fleeing the scene of the crime, obviously in a hurry to escape the consequences of her actions."

Fletcher countered, "Objection, your honor. The prosecution has no way of knowing my client's motives."

"Sustained," Justice Grimshaw said.

"Chief Ferguson," the prosecutor continued, "did the defendant at any time admit to leaving the gas station without paying?"

The chief said, "Yes, she did say—"

"A simple yes or no is sufficient."

"Yes."

"No further questions, your honor."

Fletcher then asked, "Chief Ferguson, did my client explain *why* she temporarily left the premises before completing her transaction?"

"Yes, sir," Chief Ferguson said. "She said that the gas station wouldn't take credit cards and that she and her friend didn't have enough cash, so they went looking for an ATM."

"No further questions for this witness, your honor."

The prosecutor asked for a follow-up question. "Chief Ferguson, how long have you been a police officer?"

"Thirty-two years."

"And in your thirty-two years as a law enforcement officer, would you say that you have become a good judge of whether people are telling the truth or not?"

"Yes, sir."

"So as a thirty-two-year veteran of the force, in your professional opinion, when Miss White said she left the gas station without paying in order to..." The prosecutor made air quotes with his fingers. "...*find an ATM machine...* was she telling the truth?"

"No."

"Objection!" Fletcher said.

"Overruled." The justice countered.

"No more questions, your honor," the prosecutor said, strutting back to his seat with a satisfied smile.

Jennifer felt a stab of fear in her chest. She should've known she wouldn't get away with it. What was she thinking?

Fletcher leaned down and whispered to Jennifer.

"Would the defense like to call any witnesses?" Justice Grimshaw asked.

Fletcher continued to whisper with his client.

"Mr. Fletcher, the court asked you a question."

"Are you sure you can do this?" he asked Jennifer. She nodded.

Fletcher straightened. "Your honor, the defense would like to call Miss Jennifer Ann White to the stand."

The gallery oohed and aahed.

Judge Grimshaw pounded his gavel and called for order.

Jennifer slowly walked to the witness box and took a seat. Her legs felt like rubber. The bailiff brought out the Holy Bible again and held it out to Jennifer. Placing her hand on top, she repeated after the bailiff, "Eye for an eye, tooth for a tooth, I swear to tell the absolute truth, so help me God."

The skilled defender guided his client through recounting her story of how the gas station clerk refused to take her credit card and then proceeded to solicit her for sex in exchange.

The women in the gallery gasped.

Ralph took out his handkerchief and wiped his brow.

Jennifer proceeded to give her version of how she drove off to find an ATM, with every intention of returning to pay, while also fleeing to avoid Mr Tucker exacting payment in the way of unwanted sexual favors.

After she finished, Jennifer felt she'd performed well while doing her best to project an air of innocence.

"Thank you for your brave and honest answers, Miss White," Fletcher said. "I can only imagine how difficult this ordeal must've been for you."

Jennifer gazed up at the justice with her most irresistible pout. She was starting to feel confident that she might actually beat this. But then a twinge of doubt crept in, seeing that Grimshaw's bushy-browed scowl wasn't softening.

"Miss White." The prosecutor's voice startled her. "Can you show the court your receipt for the gasoline you put into your car?"

"I already told everyone, I tried to pay—"

"Did you lose the receipt, Miss White?"

"No, like I said—"

"Isn't it true Miss White, that the reason you cannot present the receipt for the gas you put in your car, is because you never paid for it?"

"I couldn't—"

"No further questions, your honor." The prosecutor pushed his glasses up on his nose, punctuating his final argument.

Jennifer returned to her seat, her confidence waning.

The attorneys presented their closing arguments as she chewed her lip, her stomach doing flip-flops. Once the lawyers finished, she and Latisha clasped hands.

"Will the defendant, Jennifer Ann White, please stand?" the Justice announced.

Jennifer squirmed in her seat.

"On the charge of one count speeding fifteen miles over the limit, I find the defendant... guilty."

Jennifer sighed. She'd expected to be found guilty of speeding and driving without a seatbelt. She wasn't surprised by either verdict.

The justice continued, "On the charges of one count each petty theft and fleeing the scene of a crime, I find the defendant..."

Latisha squeezed Jennifer's hand just as Fletcher put his hand on her shoulder.

"...guilty!"

The gallery erupted behind them. Jennifer stole a look over her shoulder to see the toothless old man in the overalls dancing a jig and whooping it up. "Give 'em the chair!" he shouted repeatedly.

The crowd chanted, "Bring out the chair! Bring out the chair!"

Judge Grimshaw pounded his gavel to restore order.

The gallery grew silent.

"Mr. Fletcher, are your clients prepared to settle their debt?"

Fletcher whispered so only his clients could hear. "Your fines shouldn't be more than a couple hundred dollars. If you think you need more time to raise the money..."

"If they'll take a credit card," Jennifer said, "I'd just as soon pay now so we can get the hell out of this place. No offense."

"None taken." Fletcher stood to address the court. "I believe my clients are prepared to settle their debts, your honor."

The justice nodded and asked Latisha to rise. "To settle your debt to society for committing seven counts of moral turpitude, I sentence you... to the chair, ad septem exodontia." Grimshaw punctuated the sentence with a slam of his gavel.

"What the—" Latisha turned to her attorney.

"Bailiff?" Grimshaw said. "Ready the chair."

Latisha's jaw dropped.

The crowd erupted in cheers as the bailiff strode over to the corner of the courtroom to a large rectangular object covered in a dusty canvas tarp. Jennifer hadn't noticed it was there until now.

The justice silenced the gallery again with his gavel.

With a bit of a flourish, the bailiff grabbed hold of the tarp and swept it away to reveal what appeared to be an antique barber chair.

* * *

The bailiff turned toward Latisha, hitched up his gun belt, and advanced toward her. Latisha started to retreat before running into a solid wall of flesh. Chief Ferguson looked down at her, and just as she attempted to escape, he grabbed her arm and reeled her in.

"Get yo hands off me!"

Latisha fought to pull away, but the chief's vice-like grip clamped tighter. Her pulse throbbed in her arm from the pressure. Latisha made a fist and cocked it back to clock the chief. The bailiff arrived just in time to grab her arm in mid-swing.

She struggled and kicked as the two officers dragged her toward the chair. Latisha gave it her best, but the two men overpowered her. Chief Ferguson pushed her into the barber chair and held her down while the bailiff cinched her wrists to the chair's arms with thick leather straps.

Latisha had never felt this helpless in her life. Her mind reeled, imagining the kinds of torture they had planned for her.

Just then, a side door opened, and the brawny mustachioed man they'd seen smoking in front of the barbershop entered. With him, he carried a large, black leather bag.

"Your honor." The Barber said, giving the judge a nod and setting the bag on a rustic-looking table next to the barber chair. The table looked like it had seen some action, its surface covered in nicks and divots and quite possibly claw marks.

Latisha watched in wide-eyed terror as The Barber retrieved a leather apron spattered with reddish-brown stains and slipped it over his head like a clergyman donning his vestment. After removing a black leather case from the bag, he set it on the table and unfolded it, revealing what appeared to be a set of medical instruments.

Latisha's eyes nearly bulged out of their sockets.

The Barber rolled his shirtsleeves to the elbow, revealing thick forearms covered in course black hair. He rubbed his massive hands together as if he was going to enjoy this. After carefully selecting the proper tool, The Barber turned toward Latisha and held up a metal instrument resembling a crooked pair of pliers.

"Aw, hell no!" Latisha shouted.

The bailiff said, "The less you fight, ma'am, the sooner it will all be over."

The Barber spread the jaws of the instrument and leaned over Latisha. "Open wide."

Latisha spat in his face.

The Barber wiped her spittle from his cheek and grinned. Light glinted off his gold tooth. He grabbed a fistful of Latisha's hair and pinned her head to the headrest, then brought the instrument to within a centimeter of her eye. "Eye for an eye or tooth for a tooth... don't much matter to me."

Latisha's vision blurred, and she felt a hot trickle down her cheek. She tested the wrist straps. The leather bit into her flesh but refused to give. She had never backed away from a fight in her life, but this time, she could see no escape.

She steeled herself for the inevitable, vowing not to weep or beg. No way would she give them the satisfaction.

"That's a good girl," The Barber purred.

If looks could kill, she'd be burning holes through The Barber's face.

He raised the instrument to Latisha's tightly pursed lips and waited for them to part. She pinched her lips together defiantly. No one said she had to make it easy for the bastard.

The Barber grinned and brought the instrument back to her eye, then opened its jaws and forced it into her eye socket.

Latisha screamed.

The justice slammed his gavel. "Jack!"

The Barber backed off.

"You know the rules, Jack," the justice said.

The Barber returned to his bag of tricks and retrieved what looked like a blackjack. He nodded to the bailiff, who grabbed her head from behind and pinned it back against the headrest.

With Latisha unable to twist her head and avoid the pliers, The Barber pinched her nostrils shut. Her adrenaline surging, Latisha fought bravely but ultimately had to gasp for air. The Barber quickly shoved the leather cudgel into her mouth sideways, tearing at the corners of her mouth as he wedged her jaw open. She nearly gagged on the bitter leather.

With his free hand, The Barber opened the jaws of the crooked pliers and leaned in closer.

Latisha felt the metal instrument clamp down on her tooth. The muscles in The Barber's forearm tensed as he squeezed the instrument and slowly cranked on the tooth to loosen it. A white flash of pain blinded her for a moment, like a flash grenade exploding in her skull. The pressure on the nerve sent shock waves through her body.

She gripped the arms of the barber chair, her fingernails digging into the wood. Her back arched against the pain as her tooth creaked in its socket like a rusty nail being pried from a two-by-four.

In one quick motion, The Barber yanked out her tooth by the root. Warm blood filled her mouth with the salty taste of copper.

Bloody drool ran down Latisha's chin as The Barber turned to the gallery and held up the prize. Cheers erupted from the audience. The toothless man in the overalls giggled and danced a jig.

The justice banged his gavel and half-heartedly said to the gallery, "Okay, okay, people. Settle down."

Latisha looked over at Jennifer whose face was in her hands, weeping. This had to be a nightmare. Surely, she'd fallen asleep in the passenger seat of Jennifer's Prius and would awaken any moment.

She managed to spit out the bloody cudgel and flex her jaw. Latisha probed inside her mouth with her tongue, discovering the gaping hole where her front tooth used to be.

At least the nightmare, real or dreamt, was over. The town had exacted (or extracted) their revenge, and she'd *paid her debt to society*. Latisha couldn't wait to get out of this hick town and find a real lawyer to sue their asses off. And then she would own this town.

When The Barber turned back, Latisha anxiously waited for him to loosen her arm straps. Instead, he looked to the justice.

"How many counts was there again, your honor?" The Barber asked.

"Seven."

The Barber grinned at Latisha and raised his eyebrows.

Not only wasn't this nightmare over, it had only just begun.

* * *

By the time The Barber extracted the seventh tooth from Latisha's mouth, she appeared utterly broken. Jennifer had never seen her friend like this. Latisha was the strongest person she'd ever known. Her friend had survived a brutal childhood. Her birth father had bailed when she was two. After that, her mother had entertained a revolving door of abusive men, at least two of which had victimized Latisha.

Despite her mother's lifelong struggle with addiction, Latisha had stayed clean. What would have broken most people had only made her stronger and more determined. But seeing her now made Jennifer wonder if someone had ultimately found a way to break her for good.

Jennifer trembled as she gazed at Latisha slumped in the barber chair, her eyes glazed over, blood drooling down her slack jaw.

The Barber dropped the last tooth into a metal container on the table with a clank and then wiped the extraction instrument on his bloodstained apron.

The bailiff came and unbuckled Latisha from the chair. When he reached to help her up, she shrugged him off and stood under her own power, her legs shaking. After a couple steps, her knees buckled. But when the bailiff again offered his assistance, she yanked her arm away and staggered toward Jennifer under her own power before collapsing into the seat next to her.

Tears streaming down her face, Jennifer stared at her friend in horror. She couldn't help but feel like she was somehow responsible. If only she hadn't gotten off at the wrong exit...

Justice Grimshaw commanded Jennifer to rise for sentencing.

"To settle your debt to society for the crimes you've committed, one count driving fifteen miles over the legal limit and one count driving without a seatbelt, I sentence you to pay a fine of $200.00."

At this point, Jennifer was willing to pay anything just to make this nightmare end.

"For the crimes of one count each petty theft and fleeing the scene of a crime, I sentence you... to the chair, pro manu, remotionem."

The justice slammed his gavel sealing Jennifer's fate.

A clamor arose from the gallery even louder than before.

The judge cried out, "Order! Order in this court!"

Jennifer's head spun as the bailiff escorted her to the barber chair. She knew fighting would be futile and would merely prolong the torture.

Her whole body seemed numb. The bailiff had her arms cinched to the chair before she realized it. As she steeled herself for The Barber and his bloodstained pliers, he instead returned to his black bag for a different instrument.

To Jennifer's surprise, The Barber retrieved an old-fashioned iron with a wood handle and a braided power cord. She watched in horror as he plugged the cord into a nearby outlet, temporarily causing the lights to dim. Her mind reeled, trying to imagine what manner of torture The Barber had in store for her.

The Barber hummed as he watched the iron heat up, filling the room with an acrid, burnt-metallic smell.

Once the tarnished iron glowed red, The Barber picked it up and spat on the steaming metal, grinning as the saliva sizzled and popped.

Jennifer began to hyperventilate.

"Not the face," she whimpered. "Please, not the face."

The Barber inexplicably set the iron back on the table and then returned to his bag of tricks. This time, he retrieved a hatchet. The blade was covered in a dark patina except for the edge, which appeared to have been honed razor-sharp. The Barber thumbed the blade and smiled with satisfaction.

Approaching the chair, he rested the hatchet blade on Jennifer's wrist, lining up the cut.

"Nooo!" Latisha shouted as she rushed the chair.

But before she could reach Jennifer, Chief Ferguson grabbed Latisha around the waist. She flailed and screamed in a last-ditch effort to save her friend, but it was too late.

The Barber raised the hatchet and slammed it down, severing Jennifer's hand in one clean chop. The appendage tumbled to the floor, hitting with a dull thud. Blood squirted onto The Barber's apron as Jennifer stared at her hemorrhaging stump in disbelief. The room closed in around her as everything faded to black.

Searing pain from the glowing metal shocked Jennifer back to consciousness. Her flesh sizzled and smoked as The Barber cauterized the wound with his iron. Breathing in the stench of her own burning flesh acted like smelling salts, bringing Jennifer fully to her senses. Staring down at her smoldering stump brought out a primal scream. The white-hot pain was so intense it made the room spin.

Chief Ferguson struggled to corral Latisha when she turned and raked her nails down the side of his face. The chief temporarily released his grip and brought his hand to his cheek. Seeing the blood on his fingers, his expression darkened. Then, in a flash, he swung his other hand across so hard that he slapped Latisha off her feet.

As the chief bent to subdue her, Latisha sprung up and drove her shoulder into his gut like an open-field tackle, knocking the wind out of him.

Gasping for breath, the chief seized Latisha by the shoulders and pulled her face up to his. Before he could utter a word, Latisha pressed the cold barrel of the chief's revolver under his chin.

Wide-eyed and drooling blood, Latisha spat the words in his face, "Black lives matter, mother fucker!" She pulled the trigger, and the Chief's eye exploded in a crimson spray as the bullet exited his orbital socket and blew a hole in the ceiling above.

Chief Ferguson collapsed in a heap at Latisha's feet like a controlled demolition.

Screams and shouts of anger rose from the gallery. As the initial shock wore off, the crowd morphed into a mob and rushed Latisha.

She managed to hold them at bay with the chief's revolver, creating space as she backed toward Jennifer, still strapped in the chair.

Jennifer yelled, "Look out!"

Latisha spun just as The Barber came at her with the bloody hatchet. He swung the blade down, chopping deep into her left shoulder just as she squeezed off two rounds center mass.

The Barber dropped to his knees and gaped at the blood leaking from the smoldering bullet holes in his leather apron. He glowered up at Latisha before his eyes rolled up into his head, and he collapsed backward.

Jennifer leaned over and bit down on the leather strap securing her remaining hand to the chair and tugged, hoping to release the prong from the strap. If she just got that hand loose, she could free her other arm.

Latisha, her head cocked to one side from the hatchet still embedded in her shoulder, turned to the bailiff. He fumbled to retrieve his gun from its holster.

She tried to raise the revolver with both hands, but the hatchet wound made her left arm practically useless. Aiming the gun with her shaky right hand, she pulled the trigger.

The shot echoed throughout the courtroom.

Wood paneling splintered behind the bailiff. He ducked and frantically managed to wrestle his revolver from its holster. He crouched in a shooter's stance, leveling his weapon.

Latisha's next bullet struck the bailiff in the face before he could squeeze the trigger, painting the wall behind him with blood and brain matter. The bailiff crumpled to the floor like a marionette with its strings cut.

The clamor from the townsfolk crescendoed, seeing another of their own fall to the outsider.

"She killed the Chief!"

"Jack was just doing his job!"

"She's got the blood of three men on her hands!"

"Put her back in the chair!"

Someone in the back shouted, "Get her!"

They charged Latisha again. She spun and leveled the service revolver at the crowd, halting them in their tracks. The men seemed to be gauging their odds of taking her down before she could get off another round.

Jennifer, her teeth locked onto the leather restraint, pulled with all her strength. The tendons in her neck strained under her pale skin. The leather creaked, cinching her arm even tighter, cutting off the circulation. With a final jerk of her neck, the metal tine popped out of the hole in the strap, freeing her arm. A rush of relief washed over her. Jennifer hastily loosened the strap securing her amputated arm.

She was free!

Jennifer scanned the mayhem around her. With all the attention on Latisha brandishing the chief's revolver, everyone seemed to have forgotten about her. Surveying the room for an exit, she finally spotted a door behind the bailiff's motionless body.

The crowd continued to advance, pushing Latisha back toward Jennifer. She spat blood on the floor between them as if drawing a red line in the sand. "If you all don't back the fuck up, I'm gonna start cappin' yo asses one at a time!"

Without anything to defend herself, and the crowd pressing in, Jennifer made a break for the door.

She hesitated as she reached the bailiff, seeing the pool of blood growing beneath his head. His eyes stared blankly at her over the bloody hole in his cheek. Was he dead? Paralyzed? Or only temporarily stunned?

Jennifer struggled to work up the nerve to step over the bailiff's body. If this were a horror movie, this is where he'd pop up and grab her.

"Please be dead. Please be dead," she whispered as she carefully stepped over the bailiff's body.

Someone shouted from the crowd, "Y'all gonna wish you never came here!"

"I said, back... the fuck... up!" Latisha shouted.

Clearing the bailiff, Jennifer glanced back at the angry throng closing in and backing Latisha toward her. Jennifer grimaced at the sight of Latisha's head canted awkwardly to one side, the hatchet blade still buried in her shoulder, her shirt soaked a dark crimson. Latisha was running out of room, and they were both running out of time.

Jennifer spun back toward the exit and slipped in the bailiff's blood, flailing her arms for balance, nearly landing on her rear. Surveying the closed door, she whispered, "Please don't be locked."

Time came to a standstill as she reached for the doorknob with her truncated wrist. How could she turn the doorknob without a hand? And why was there no hand where it's supposed to be?

Latisha glanced back at Jennifer, still gawking at the door, and shouted, "Jen! Open the fucking door!"

Jennifer studied her remaining hand. Her brain synapses began to fire again, instructing it to reach for the doorknob.

The mob pressed in.

"Jen!" Latisha shouted.

"Eye for an eye!" came a shout from the crowd.

Jennifer grasped the doorknob and turned it.

The chanting horde grew louder. "Eye for an eye! Eye for an eye!"

She felt the cylinder turn and the latch bolt retreat. *Yes!* Jennifer pushed the door. But it wouldn't budge. *No!* They'd come too far to fail now.

In a fit of rage, Jennifer threw her shoulder into the door.

It opened!

Jennifer looked back at Latisha pointing the sheriff's pistol in a townsperson's face.

"I'll fucking do it!" Latisha spat.

"Latisha!" Jennifer shouted over the clamor, "Let's go!"

Latisha turned toward Jennifer, wild-eyed and ready to bolt through the door. As she opened her mouth to respond, a thunderclap echoed through the courtroom, and everything devolved into slow motion.

Latisha's head exploded in a violent spray of brain matter and skull shrapnel.

Jennifer's mind shut out all ambient sound as if she'd been plunged underwater, barely able to hear her own scream.

The mob froze, staring in shock, buying Jennifer precious seconds.

The life drained from Latisha's eyes, yet they continued to stare at Jennifer, confused.

Why did you let this happen to me, Jennifer?

Her body crumpled to the floor overtop the bailiff's body. A sickening thud resounded as what was left of Latisha's head bounced off the floor.

Justice Grimshaw stood on the bench, pointing a smoldering .44 magnum.

Jennifer lingered in the doorway, a statue, gawking at her friend sprawled out on the floor, blood gushing from the gaping hole in her head.

Latisha's sightless eyes glared up at Jennifer.

An image of the rabbit she'd run over with its eye bulging from its socket flashed in Jennifer's mind. It then morphed back into Latisha's wide-eyed glare once again. Accusing. Her bloody lips mouthed the words *Why Jennifer? Why didn't you save me?*

Latisha's lifeblood spread across the linoleum. Once the blood reached the toe of her white leather sneaker, ambient sound crept back into her consciousness. It started with the courtroom clock ticking off the seconds, followed by shoes scuffling on linoleum. And then, the stillness was broken by a lone, muted voice, seemingly from some distant shore.

"Hoowee! Judge Grimshaw!" shouted the toothless old man. "Judge, jury, and executioner!"

Then, like a dam bursting, a cacophony of sound rushed in — the clamor of an angry mob punctuated by the judge's gavel hammering the bench. Reality rushed at Jennifer like a runaway semi-truck.

The geezer bounded toward the barber chair and scrambled to collect Latisha's teeth off the bloodstained floor, stashing the gruesome mementos into the pockets of his overalls.

Jennifer needed to act quickly before the horde of townspeople did. Or the judge decided to level his .44 magnum at her.

With a final farewell glance at her dead friend, Jennifer noticed the chief's revolver still in Latisha's hand. It was almost as if she were offering it to Jennifer, telling her to take it and save herself.

The mob regained its fury.

Jennifer's time was up.

She dropped to her knees, the warm pool of blood soaking through her capris.

Her hand trembling, Jennifer carefully pried Latisha's clammy fingers from the gun, careful not to cause the finger inside the trigger guard to discharge the firearm.

As she palmed the weapon, she was surprised at how heavy it was. Jennifer had never held a gun before, let alone shot one. She prayed she wouldn't have to.

Jennifer scrambled to her feet and backed toward the exit.

The townspeople charged.

In a moment of panic, Jennifer raised the gun toward the ceiling and fired. The force of the recoil was so startling that she flinched, nearly dropping the weapon.

The gunshot also startled the mob, buying her precious seconds.

Jennifer backpedaled from the crowd and stumbled into the hallway, right into Deputy Jacobs.

The officer grabbed her by the shoulders.

This can't be happening! To be this close, and yet... Jennifer struggled to free herself. She had to escape this nightmare.

The deputy glanced over Jennifer's shoulder, his eyes growing wide as saucers. He shoved her aside just in time to intercept the first townie coming through the door and stiff-armed the man in the chest, knocking him back into the onrushing crowd. Jacobs slammed the door and pressed his back against it, barely keeping the horde at bay.

Jennifer's heart nearly stopped, seeing Officer Jacobs reach toward his holster. Was he going to arrest her? Shoot her? Was Jennifer prepared to shoot first?

She raised the revolver as Jacobs reached into his pocket, retrieved something, and tossed it to her. With her only remaining hand already gripping the revolver, the object bounce off her chest and onto the ground.

"It's parked out back," the deputy said. "Go!"

Jennifer gawked at her car keys lying on the ground.

Jacobs lurched forward as the angry crowd tried to force the door open behind him.

"I can't hold them off for long," Jacobs shouted. "Just go!"

Jennifer shoved the gun into her waistband and retrieved the keys from the floor. With tears welling in her eyes, she mouthed, "Thank you," then sprinted down the hall.

* * *

Jennifer burst through the back exit and into the night. She scanned the sparsely lit parking lot for her car. Did everyone in this town drive a pickup? Where was her Prius? She glanced over her shoulder, expecting a lynch mob to explode through the courthouse doors any minute.

As she zig-zagged through the lot, it seemed like even the vehicles that weren't pickups were full-size gas-guzzlers. Just when she was about to give up hope, there it was, eclipsed in the shadow of a jacked-up 4x4 pickup with a *Don't Tread on Me* flag mounted on the back. Jennifer fumbled through her keyring for the key fob, but it was difficult with only one hand. Now that her adrenaline was waning, her cauterized stump was on fire.

The courthouse door crashed open, and a horde of angry townsfolk spilled out. Startled by the clamor, Jennifer dropped the keys.

"Shit!"

She crouched to pick up the keys and kept low, hoping the mob wouldn't spot her. Rummaging one-handed through her keys, she finally managed to locate the key fob and trigger the unlock button. The horn beeped, and lights flashed.

"Hey! She's over here!" someone shouted.

Jennifer lunged for the door handle with the wrong hand and jammed her stump into the door. A lightning bolt of pain shot up her arm. Stifling a cry, she pulled the handle with her lone hand.

"There she is!" someone called.

Jennifer dove into the front seat.

When she peeked over the dash to check the situation, a local wearing a brown flannel shirt and a green John Deere cap stepped in front of her car and slammed his hands on the hood.

Jennifer screamed.

The townie dashed toward Jennifer's open driver's side door.

She started for the handle with her stump-hand, then screamed in frustration. Jennifer quickly reached across her body with her only hand and grabbed the armrest a split-second before the man could get a solid grip on the doorframe. Jennifer wrenched the door free before he got a solid grip. The door slammed with a whomp, muffling his frustrated yell.

Jennifer groped for the door lock.

The man yanked the door handle just as the electric locks depressed with a loud *click-clunk*. Her pursuer pounded the driver's side window with his palm.

Jennifer screamed and frantically pressed the Power button. The console glowed to life, and the seatbelt alarm chimed.

The local continued to tug on the door handle, rocking the Prius.

Jennifer jammed the vehicle into reverse and punched the accelerator without even looking behind her. The only thought screaming in her head was to get the hell out of there. *Now.*

Something thumped off her back bumper. Checking the rearview mirror, she saw a man spin and hit the ground. Jennifer stomped the brakes.

"Oh-my-God! Oh-my-God!" What had she done? She grabbed the door handle to get out and check on the person she had struck, then paused.

What if she just killed one of the locals? They cut off her hand just for stealing a tank of gas; imagine what they do to murderers!

An image flashed in her mind of her ankles being chained to the bumper of Ralph's tow truck.

Ralph, craning his head out the window with a half-smoked cigar chomped between his teeth, grinning. The diesel engine revving. Jennifer screaming as the tow truck spun its tires, spewing gravel in the air and dragging her down the street to howls of delight from the townies.

Latisha's voice echoed in her mind, "Just go! Go, go, go!"

Jennifer shifted into drive and gunned it, the front tires spitting gravel, clinking and clanking against the undercarriage.

A guy with a baseball bat rushed her car and shattered the passenger side window. She screamed as shards of glass exploded across her lap, tiny pieces biting into her cheek.

The bat-wielding townie reached through the window and unlocked the door just as the tires finally gained traction. He pulled the passenger door open just as the Prius lurched forward. The car door slammed into the man, the momentum forcing the door shut as she sped toward the exit.

A middle-aged man in a suit, tie, and fedora stepped in front of Jennifer's car, motioning her to stop. Jennifer stomped the accelerator to the floorboard. The suit dove at the last moment, his knee slamming off the fender.

Reaching the parking lot exit, Jennifer's car bottomed out, her muffler scraping the street and spraying sparks. She accelerated out of the turn and raced onto Main Street.

Part of the agitated throng had exited the courthouse through the front and wandered into the street. A hefty woman stepped into her path, forcing Jennifer to swerve to avoid hitting her. The Prius jumped the curb, forcing Jennifer to straddle the sidewalk.

A teenage boy's face flashed terror. He dove out of her way at the last second, only to expose a telephone pole.

Jennifer screamed and cranked the wheel, bouncing back onto Main Street and narrowly avoiding a parked car.

Glancing in her rearview mirror, she saw Main Street filling with townsfolk. The only thing missing were their torches and pitchforks.

Jennifer glimpsed a stop sign ahead.

And a pedestrian.

"Shit!" Jennifer stomped the brake, her tires screeching.

She still struck the pedestrian, driving him face-first into the hood.

The pedestrian pushed himself up and into the glare of her headlights. He looked like he'd stepped out of the fifties with his receding hairline, long sideburns, and the pack of cigarettes rolled up in his shirt sleeve. She wondered if she had gone through a time warp as she searched for answers to this neverending nightmare.

The irate pedestrian slammed his hands on the hood, startling Jennifer.

Before she knew what was happening, others appeared around her car, banging on the windows and the roof. The Prius started rocking. *They're going to tip it over!*

A thick, hairy arm reached through her shattered passenger-side window, the meaty hand grasping her sleeve.

Jennifer panicked and flattened the accelerator to the floor.

The wounded pedestrian face-planted onto the hood, blocking her view of the road ahead. His expression turned from anger to fear and back to anger again.

The hand gripping her sleeve tugged at her, but as she accelerated, forcing the intruder to let go or be dragged down the street.

Gasping for breath, Jennifer's blindly sped down the street.

The man on the hood held on for dear life, pounding on the glass with his free hand, trying to make Jennifer stop. Unable to see, a horrific thought occurred to her. What if she was speeding toward a tree or a light post? Hell, for all she knew, she might be about to careen over a cliff. Jennifer knew she had to shake this guy. But if she stopped, the mob might catch up to her and—

Jennifer swerved to the left. Her unwelcome passenger's lower body swung like a pendulum, but he managed to hold on. She swerved to the right. But still couldn't shake him. He pounded his fist into the windshield, startling her, and created a spider web crack.

Her chest tightened as the landscape rushed by her side windows, the pedestrian still blinding her to the dangers that lay ahead. The man smashed the windshield again, expanding the crack.

Cutting the wheel back and forth failed to jar him loose. He raised his fist to strike the windshield again. Jennifer had to try something more drastic before it was too late. At this point, what did she have to lose?

Tires screeched as she locked up the brakes, her front end nosediving toward the pavement as the Prius came to an abrupt stop.

The pedestrian launched through the air backward. In Jennifer's mind, time slowed to a crawl. Details became increasingly vivid. Like the shock on the man's face, the way he grasped at the air as if suddenly untethered from a space capsule... floating... drifting into an infinite void.

Then, time and space caught up with him as he struck the pavement. His head bounced off the blacktop, and his body turned into a ragdoll, skipping and tumbling, before finally skidding face-first to an abrupt stop.

Jennifer struggled to catch her breath as she stared at the motionless pile of flesh and bone before her, waiting for it to move.

Was he dead?

A shout came from behind her.

Jennifer checked the rearview mirror. In the distance, more townsfolk gathered in the street, shouting and pointing in her direction. An elderly man wagged his cane in her direction as if leading the charge into battle.

The mob marched toward her.

Jennifer released the brake and accelerated, hoping to put some distance between her and the approaching mob. She steered to the left to avoid the motionless pedestrian and the red streak staining the road where he'd skidded to a stop.

The image of the squashed rabbit flashed in her mind — the blood trail, the tread mark across its abdomen that turned its insides out. Jennifer quickly shook the image from her head. But her eyes returned to the blood-streaked pavement and the man lying face-down in the street.

As her car reached the body, he slowly raised his head.

He's alive!

But Jennifer's relief was short-lived. As the Prius crawled alongside the wounded pedestrian, he lifted his head and turned toward her, revealing that one whole side of his face was scraped down to the bone. Strips of flesh hung loosely from his skull. His jaw hung unhinged, teeth exposed in a perverse grin.

Oh, God! What have I done?

Angry shouts behind her grew closer. A rock ricocheted off her rear window, startling Jennifer into action. She wrenched her gaze from the horror in the street and punched the accelerator.

Faster.

Faster!

Little by little, the wretched town shrunk in her rearview mirror, eventually fading from view.

Ghostly farmland raced past in a blur.

Jennifer checked the rearview mirror again. The road was empty.

A low fog rolled across the fields and crawled across the road as if the town was reaching for her with its ghostly tendrils, attempting to seize hold of her and drag her back, kicking and screaming.

As the fog thickened, the Prius seemed to slow. It was as if the sinister mist had seeped into the engine and gummed up the works. Jennifer imagined the engine and drivetrain rusting and seizing up before stopping altogether, the thick fog enveloping her in its deadly embrace.

Then, a ray of hope pierced through the haze. The freeway! A relic from a world she used to know. Could it be? Or was it just a mirage, mocking her?

And then, another breadcrumb of reality. A distant memory materialized off the side of the road, the familiar overgrown sign with the faded hand-painted arrow that started it all, pointing her back to the horrors she fled.

A spike of fear tempered with cautious optimism surged through Jennifer at the sight of the entrance ramp, an oasis in the middle of a desert. Jennifer blinked away the tears blurring her vision, and turned onto the highway.

* * *

Jennifer drove through the veil of darkness, her thoughts scattered, operating on auto-pilot. She had no idea where she was or where she was going. The adrenaline dump from her escape left her completely drained. Numb. The only sounds invading the car were the monotonous drone of the tires and the roaring headwinds.

A voice deep down prodded Jennifer to make a U-turn and head back home. To not stop until she was back in the safety of her mother's arms. Or maybe if she pinched herself, she might awaken from this unfathomable nightmare. Then she glanced down at her still amputated wrist. How could she pinch herself without fingers?

Jennifer stifled a sob.

The serene road hum from her tires gradually grew as if someone was turning up the volume. Or was that the drone of a second, louder, larger set of tires creeping up on her?

At first, the thought of someone else on the road with her provided a sense of comfort. She considered rolling down her window and waving them down. A shrill laugh escaped her, imagining their reaction when they saw her handless wave.

The glare of headlights in her rearview mirror confirmed the presence of another vehicle.

Jennifer shifted in her seat, sitting up a little straighter. She glanced at the speedometer, just in case it was a state trooper wondering what she was doing on the road at this hour. Jennifer noticed she was driving 13 mph over the speed limit and eased her foot off the accelerator.

The vehicle behind her sped up. High beams flooded the Prius's interior as if it were daylight. A jolt of terror made her jump, fearing that she was about to get pulled over for speeding. But then she thought, *would that really be such a bad thing*? If it was the state police, she could tell them about the medieval hick town that tortured wayward travelers. And maybe seek justice for herself and Latisha. Her heart ached, thinking of her best friend still lying on the courtroom floor in a pool of blood.

As the road noise amplified, Jeniffer recognized the rattling roar of that diesel engine closing in behind her.

The sound a tow truck might make.

A loud thud and crunching plastic shattered the night. Jennifer's neck snapped back and bounced off the headrest as the tow truck rammed her from behind. Good Lord, hadn't these people inflicted enough damage already?

The diesel roared as the tow truck accelerated and slammed into Jennifer again, propelling the Prius forward. It was all she could do to maintain control with only one hand on the steering wheel. She temporarily swerved onto the gravel shoulder before correcting.

Jennifer mashed the pedal to the floor, but deep down, she knew her Prius would never outrun the tow truck's superior horsepower, especially with that madman behind the wheel.

The tow truck's engine growled, then swerved into the adjacent lane.

Jennifer screamed at the top of her lungs. Even with the accelerator pressed to the floor, the tow truck continued to gain ground, finally pulling even with her.

"Go, you piece of shit!" Jennifer yelled, banging the steering wheel with her fist.

She could feel the truck driver's glare. Jennifer stole a glance at the truck and confirmed her worst fear — *Ralph's Towing Service.*

The truck swerved right and slammed into Jennifer's Prius, crushing her side-view mirror and forcing her onto the gravel shoulder. She wrestled the steering wheel with her one hand, gripping it so hard her knuckles turned white. Gravel battered the undercarriage as she steered the vehicle back onto the road.

Ralph cut his wheel and rammed the car again, forcing her back onto the shoulder. Her side-view mirror dangled by a cable, knocking against the door panel. She imagined a wild-eyed Ralph pounding on her car door, taunting, *"Little pig, little pig, let me in!"*

Jennifer tried to return to the highway, but Ralph's truck had her boxed out.

A highway marker rushed toward her. With Ralph matching her speed, Jennifer had to make a split-second decision — run head-on into the sign or swerve offroad down the embankment.

She swerved.

Dry brush scraped the undercarriage as the Prius bucked over the uneven terrain. The steering wheel jerked violently back and forth, yanking it from her grip. Jennifer crushed the brake pedal until she finally managed to bring the vehicle to an abrupt stop. Her body pitched forward, the seatbelt practically clotheslining her, but narrowly saved her face from smashing into the windshield.

The Prius's headlights illuminated a dust cloud of debris, stifling her field of vision. As the dust cleared, she took stock of herself. Aside from her racing heart, possibly bruised upper chest, and likely whiplash, she seemed relatively intact. The vehicle was another story. Her driver's side door was smashed in; the side mirror hung limp. She feared what kind of damage the undercarriage incurred and prayed the vehicle was still driveable.

Just when her pulse began to return to normal, bright spotlights shone from the highway — but they seemed to be driving the wrong way.

Jennifer's mind rewound to earlier (yesterday?) and the sight of Ralph's tow truck reversing toward her when she and Latisha had tried to escape. She recognized the large, sun-faded red taillights and the roof-mounted spotlights.

Once again, they were coming for her.

Jennifer stomped the accelerator. The engine whined, but the front tires failed to gain traction. She shifted into reverse, but her car still wouldn't budge.

Ralph's tow truck left the freeway and barreled backward down the bumpy slope toward her. The backup spotlights bounced as the tow truck traversed the rough terrain, the hook and chain swinging wildly.

Jennifer yanked on the door handle, but the damn door refused to open. She fumbled with the door locks until she heard them click. She tried the door again. No luck. The door must've gotten jammed when the tow truck slammed into her.

The reverse spotlights drew closer. Jennifer feared that if she didn't act quickly, and he broadsided her at speed, she'd be crushed to death.

She struggled to unbuckle her seatbelt one-handed. Maybe she had enough time to free herself and escape out the passenger-side door.

But the damn thing won't unlock!

The more she writhed and struggled against her seatbelt, the more the handgun dug into her ribs.

THE REVOLVER!

The spotlights grew brighter, flooding the interior. She was running out of time.

Jennifer sucked in her stomach and slipped the revolver from her waistband.

Unable to acquire a target with the spotlights blinding her, Jennifer raised her amputated arm in a feeble attempt to shield her face from the impending impact and a shower of shattering glass.

But the impact never came.

The tow truck slammed its brakes and skidded to a stop, pelting her car with rocks and debris.

The driver's side door squeaked as the tow truck driver stepped down from the cab. His dark silhouette emerged through the dust cloud, his boots scuffing across the gravel.

Jennifer glanced down at the gun gripped tightly in her hand. There was no way she was going back to that shithole town. She'd rather die on the side of the road than be dragged back there.

The driver pulled a thick, rusty chain from the back of the tow truck, creating a discordant shriek of metal on metal. He dragged the chain across the ground as he headed toward Jennifer.

She stared at the revolver, building up her nerve.

A sick realization twisted her gut — what if she was out of bullets? How many bullets were in a gun, anyway?

And how many had already been shot?

Jennifer made a quick mental inventory.

There was the first shot when Latisha shot the police chief with his own gun. Then, the two shots fired into The Barber's chest...

The sound of the dragging chain grew closer.

...then there was the bailiff. But didn't Latisha miss once?

Closer.

Jennifer examined the number of chambers in the cylinder — Six.

If she counted right, she had one bullet left.

Jennifer's throat tightened.

The tow truck driver reached the driver's side door, blocking out the light.

I can't go back there. I just can't!

Ralph grinned through the window.

Her hand shaking, Jennifer raised the revolver and pulled the trigger.

Click...

About B.D. Prince

B.D. Prince was raised in Michigan before moving to California in his twenties to pursue screenwriting and a tan. The dark fiction and comedy writer credits these proclivities to growing up near a cemetery and being endowed with a freakishly long funny bone.

Prince got his start writing humorous greeting cards and penning one-liners for Joan Rivers. Now an award-winning author and screenwriter, Prince won the 2024 Imadjinn Award for the novel 28 Years Haunted. Having also published many short stories and novellas, B.D. Prince is currently writing a new horror novel and developing projects for film and television.

You can follow B.D. Prince at...

BDPrince.com
Instagram: @clownprinceb
Facebook: facebook.com/bryan.prince.52
Twitter/X: @clownprinceb